"You don
Somebody
these days
from your b

Zane took a deep breath, his already broad chest expanding. "I've got half a mind to marry you myself!"

The table erupted in a general outpouring of surprise, quickly followed by approval. For her part, Dara simply stared. Then it occurred to her that he was joking. She laughed weakly but the thought of this man as her husband sent a sharp jolt of excitement singing through her veins.

Welcome to ♥ Whirlwind Weddings

Whirlwind Weddings is a brand-new mini-series about matrimony, featuring strong, irresistible heroes, feisty heroines and four marriages made not so much in heaven as in a hurry!

When the authors came up with the idea for **Whirlwind Weddings** we gave them just one stipulation: their heroes and heroines had to meet and marry within a week! Mission impossible? Well, a lot can happen in seven days...

Titles in this series are:

Dear Reader

I met the man I would marry in January; we started dating in February, got serious in March; he proposed in April, and we got married in May—on a Friday the thirteenth! Maybe that's not a Whirlwind Wedding compared to Zane and Dara's dash to the altar but it was fast enough to make our nearest and dearest very nervous indeed about our chance for happiness.

As it turned out, they needn't have worried. With my husband of more than thirty years, I've learned that 'happily ever after' exists in real life as well as in fiction. May it exist in *your* real life, too.

Ruth Jean Dale

DASH TO
THE ALTAR

BY
RUTH JEAN DALE

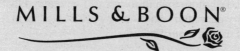

MILLS & BOON®

This book is dedicated to Margaret Brownley, a wonderful
woman who also happens to be a wonderful writer and a
wonderful friend. Boy, have we been through a lot together!
Thanks for everything, Miz B.

*First published in Great Britain 1998
Harlequin Mills & Boon Limited,
Eton House, 18-24 Paradise Road, Richmond, Surrey TW9 1SR*

© Betty Lee Duran 1998

ISBN 0 263 80744 4

*Set in Times Roman 11 on 12 pt.
02-9804-44963 C1*

*Printed and bound in Great Britain
by Mackays of Chatham PLC, Chatham*

CHAPTER ONE

ZANE Farley had heard women complain about "bad hair" days, but he was having a "bad all over" day. It started when he cut himself shaving; escalated when he discovered, just a half hour before the biggest calf-roping event of the year was set to begin, that his roping horse, Scout, had thrown a shoe; and got *real* bad when he looked up to see Jody Mitchell bearing down on him.

Jody was a professional barrel racer and just about the best-looking woman in the rodeo business, in Zane's considered opinion. He'd been dating her off and on for a couple of years, since they ran into each other frequently at the various rodeos. Nothing really serious, but he had been looking forward to renewing old acquaintances here at the National Finals Rodeo in Las Vegas.

Therefore he was understandably taken aback when she'd thrust out her arm to display a diamond on the third finger of her left hand.

"What the hell is that supposed to mean?" he growled.

"That I'm engaged," she responded tartly.

"Who to?"

"Not you! If you'd got off the dime, it *coulda* been you." She threw up her hands in a gesture of dismissal. "But that's all right—I don't take it personal!"

It sure sounded personal to Zane. "Now, Jody, calm down and—"

"Don't you tell me to calm down, Zane Farley! I'm done throwin' good time after bad where you're concerned. I'll get the last laugh, though. Someday you'll be a lonesome, beat-up old has-been and you'll *still* be lookin' for that perfect woman who'll measure up to your high-and-mighty standards." Planting her hands on her hips, she glared at him. "I'd sure like to see the woman who could tame you, cowboy, but I don't think she exists!"

With that, she'd sashayed away, swinging her hips inside those tight turquoise jeans.

So why did that annoy Zane so thoroughly? It wasn't as if he intended to marry her himself—hell, no! It wasn't as if he intended to marry *anyone* himself; she'd got that part right. Zane didn't believe in marriage, hadn't since his mother took off with another man, leaving a husband and two little boys behind. Zane had been five and his brother, Jake, just turned ten.

It wasn't something Zane talked about much, but when his mother left, she took his faith in women with her. He didn't trust any of them to hang around when the going got rough. So why did Jody's announcement tick him off so bad he went out and took 13.5 seconds to rope and tie a calf that should have hit the ground in half that? This was such an unheard-of occurrence that it made him the talk of the rodeo and the butt of a lot of ribbing, most of it good-natured.

Hours later, standing at one end of the bar of the Golden Gringo Casino and Saloon in the middle of a crowd of fellow rodeo competitors, he reached for his second beer and groaned.

"That arm still botherin' you?" the cowboy standing next to him inquired.

"Some." Zane pulled the beer in front of him, then rubbed his left elbow. "Got it yanked pretty good." Which was an understatement. When he'd tackled his critter in the steer-wrestling event, the big beast had rolled over his arm and ground it into the soft dirt of the arena. Zane knew he'd got off lucky.

"You take anything for that?"

"Nah. Didn't want to stand in line to get doctored."

"Know what you mean." The cowboy dug around in his jeans pocket and hauled out a small white envelope. "Here, I tried these when I busted my collarbone a few months back and they worked real good. Take a bunch, they're small."

Zane eyed the offering askance. "Thanks, but I believe I'll pass. Don't know what's in that stuff."

The cowboy shrugged. "How bad can it be? They come from a doctor, but suit yourself. If you change your mind, just holler."

"Thanks, but I won't change my mind. As long as I don't try to do-si-do around the dance floor, I should be all right."

At that very moment, the front door of the Golden Gringo swung open and Zane's old buddy, Slim, walked in. He was escorting the most breathtaking woman Zane Farley had ever laid eyes on. He stopped talking to stare.

She had curly blond hair that kind of spilled to her shoulders, and she wore some sort of light-colored pantsuit that clung to her like sauce on a sundae. Unaware of his avid attention, she stopped short to look around with wide eyes, as if she'd never seen a saloon before.

Maybe she hadn't. She didn't look like the kind of woman who'd frequent such places. In fact, she didn't look "country" at all. When she turned to speak to Slim, the light spilled over her and Zane caught his breath. Was that a sparkle of tears on her lashes or simply fairy dust?

Either way, he figured she'd be just the one to help him forget about Jody's...hell, Jody's disloyalty. Good old Slim would introduce them. Zane elbowed the cowboy beside him.

"I've changed my mind," he announced. "I believe I *will* try one of those pills of yours." The man obligingly produced the packet and offered several tablets, which Zane washed down with half a glass of beer.

Dara Linnell clung to the old cowboy's arm and looked around with consternation. The Golden Gringo had only two public telephones and at least a half-dozen people waited to use them. She glanced at Slim. "Maybe I should just go back outside and see if I can hail a cab," she ventured.

"Not on your tintype!" He looked indignant at the very suggestion. "The night's young and I see some friends a mine over there. Why don't we join 'em 'til one a them phones opens up?''

Dara held back, feeling completely alien to these surroundings. ''I don't know if I should intrude on your friends.'' But her gaze followed his and, as if caught by a magnetic force, settled unerringly on a man at the end of the bar. She caught her breath and her eyes widened in appreciation.

He was gorgeous. She'd never seen a man so good-looking, but not in the pretty-boy manner of so many of her acquaintances. Midnight dark hair spilled over his forehead, giving him a jaunty air. His shoulders were broad beneath a cowboy shirt and that was all she could see, what with the movement of the crowd.

It was enough.

''Oh…dear,'' she said faintly.

''Yep,'' Slim said with satisfaction. ''That's my old pal, Zane Farley. The Farleys own the Bar F, but they couldn't run it without *me,* no sirree-bob. C'mon over and lemme introduce you.''

She didn't protest, just followed him while he snaked his way through the crowd. The Golden Gringo was jumping tonight, no doubt about it, and most of the revelers were in Western attire.

A small area opened up in front of the handsome cowboy. This close, she could see that his eyes were dark, too, and his skin sun browned. His face was all strength and confidence, with smile lines bracketing a sensuous mouth. Just looking at him made her own mouth go dry.

Slim touched her elbow. ''Don't believe I caught your name, little lady.''

"It's Dara. Dara Linnell."

"In that case, Miss Dara Linnell, I wantcha to meet Zane Farley, my old saddle pard and a man to ride the river with. Zane, this here is—"

"Dara," he said, and his voice caressed her name. He reached out to take her hand in his.

Dara stared at him, mesmerized. The feel of his hand surrounding hers, possessing hers, sent shivers down her spine. Her scalp prickled and her breathing stopped. She had never met anyone who affected her so strongly, so quickly. Talk about like at first sight!

"Zane." She licked her lips. "That's an unusual name. I never knew anyone named Zane before."

His fingers tightened around her hand, not oppressively but possessively. "I was named for Zane Grey, the Western writer," he said in an attractive drawl. His gaze moved the length of her, lightly but intimately. "My guess is that you're not from around these parts, Dara."

"No." She finally came to her senses and slipped her hand from his, feeling the residual glow all the way to her elbow. It was too soon; she couldn't already be responding to another man! Calming herself, she elaborated, "I'm from San Francisco, actually."

He moved over to make standing room for her next to him at the bar. "You here for the rodeo?"

"The rodeo?" She blinked in surprise. "No. I...didn't know there *was* one."

Slim bellied up to the bar at her other side. "Just the biggest rodeo in the country is all," he boasted. "This is the national finals, girl. Only the top fifteen cowboys qualify in each event. There's millions in prize money at stake, not to mention braggin' rights.''

Slim might be talking, but her attention remained riveted upon Zane. ''You're a real cowboy?'' she murmured with a kind of awe. She didn't know there were any cowboys left outside of old Western movies.

His grin did funny things to her breathing. Blake Williams had *never* affected her this way. She felt a sudden and completely unexpected shaft of relief that she hadn't married Blake before discovering that men like this one existed.

''You can't tell by my outfit?'' he countered in a lightly teasing tone. ''You really *are* a city girl.'' He touched her elbow and she jumped as if zapped by electricity. ''What can I get you to drink? A beer all right?''

She didn't much care for beer, had never learned to enjoy it even though she'd tried. But this didn't seem like a *wine* sort of place. Besides, *he* was drinking beer. ''That will be fine,'' she agreed.

Zane gestured to the bartender. ''And then you can tell me how a nice girl like you got hooked up with an old reprobate like Slim here,'' he said still teasing.

There it was, the inquiry she would just as soon have avoided. ''Actually...'' She bit her lip, debating. In her experience, prevarication only led to trouble, so she continued firmly, ''He picked me up.''

''He—''

Slim interrupted. ''Now, Dary—you don't mind if I call you Dary, do you? Nicknames just come natural to me. Now, Dary, that's not exactly how it happened.

Truth is, that Benson boy—the young one, what's his name?''

"Tom Benson?" Zane guessed.

"Yeah, that'un. Him and some of that wild bunch he runs with come along and tried to get friendly with this little lady, so I stepped in."

The barkeep placed three beers before them and moved on. Dara cupped a hand around the middle one. "It was very kind of you, Slim, but I was in no danger." She glanced at Zane and found him watching her intently. "To be perfectly honest, Slim and I had already struck up a conversation. You see—"

"No need to go into any of that," Slim broke in. "Drink your beer, get acquainted."

"But I—"

"Have a pretzel." Slim shoved the bowl at her.

Zane chuckled. "Shut up and let the lady talk, Slim." Slim subsided, grumbling under his breath. Zane smiled encouragement. "You were telling me how you and this old cowboy met."

She nodded, looking at her beer and not at him. After tonight, she'd never see him again, but she hated to think he might go away with a poor opinion of her. "We met right out there on the sidewalk," she said. "He came up and told me I was…what was it you said, Slim? The lostest-looking thing he ever saw, I believe it was. And he was right. I was lost because…" She took a deep breath and faced Zane, trying to be strong even in her humiliation. "I came to Las Vegas to get married," she announced.

"And you got left at the altar?" An expression of horrified disbelief settled on Zane's face.

"Worse." She gave a woeful little chuckle. "I got left at the Golden Gringo."

Less than an hour earlier, Dara had been staring at the classic profile of her fiancé, Blake Williams. Tall, tanned and movie-star handsome, he had also proven himself to be attentive and romantic. But at that moment there'd been something...something *hungry* about him.

She licked her lips and looked out the window of the sleek rented convertible, blinded more by nerves than by the glitter of the Las Vegas strip near midnight.

They'd be married within the hour. She would be Mrs. Blake Williams and *then* let her grandfather try to run her life! She was twenty-five, more than old enough to make her own choices. And she chose—

The cell phone rang and she jumped a foot, her heart racing with automatic alarm. But it couldn't be her grandfather, she reassured herself; Donald Linnell thought she was in Beverly Hills visiting a friend. When she'd left San Francisco, he'd still been at his office. He might not even realize she was gone.

This was probably one of those "Welcome to Las Vegas" calls. She reached for the telephone, but Blake beat her to it, practically snatching it from her hand.

"Yes?" he said into the mouthpiece. "Uh-huh...uh-huh...that's right..." He kept his gaze straight ahead. "All right, but there's no point."

The call was obviously of no importance. Dara let her attention wander....

They'd already picked up their marriage license and were on their way to one of the multitude of wedding chapels in Las Vegas. Even though it was to her benefit, Dara had been a little shocked to discover that the Clark County, Nevada courthouse was open continuously from 8:00 a.m. Friday to midnight Sunday to issue marriage licenses: no blood tests, no waiting, no nothing. Wham, bam, thank you, ma'am!

The whole thing seemed crass and commercial and made her vaguely uneasy. She had never planned to elope anyway, although just about everyone in her family had at one time or another with disastrous consequences. Her grandfather's opposition had forced her into this. She'd always imagined she'd fly in the face of family tradition with a huge ceremony, herself the centerpiece in a beautiful white gown.

Her grandfather's smothering opposition to every independent thought and action she'd ever taken or even contemplated made that impossible. She had no choice but to elope, she rationalized.

Blake's clipped words, spoken into the cell phone, caught her wandering attention. "We're on our way to the chapel now. If you think we're going to change our plans at this late date…"

Must be one of the many salespeople to whom they'd spoken about wedding options: bungee jumping, on bicycles or on horseback or scuba diving; in a helicopter hovering five hundred feet above the city lights; in a hot-air balloon or even in a drive-through ceremony that didn't require either bride or bridegroom to so much as get out of the car.

Then there was an Elvis-impersonating minister or,

since this was December, one dressed as Santa Claus. Dara had just kept shaking her head *no*.

Blake turned off the Strip onto a side street with its own fair share of casinos and bars. Suddenly, he swerved to the curb and stopped the car, although he didn't kill the engine.

"Done," he said, and his expression changed to one of narrow-eyed relief. He punched the Off button and placed the telephone back into its cradle before lifting his gaze to meet Dara's puzzled one.

She smiled. "What is it, darling? Surely you didn't let whoever that was talk you into something undignified like—like dressing up in gorilla suits or wearing roller skates!" She laughed, realized how anxious she sounded and bit her lip.

For a moment, he simply stared at her as if he'd never seen her before. Then he said, "I'm sorry."

Her heart fluttered with alarm. "Sorry?"

"I thought if he was going to do anything, it would have been days ago."

"Do anything? Who?"

"Your grandfather."

"But...he doesn't know we're eloping. How could he?"

"He knows." Blake shifted as if unable to continue meeting her shocked gaze. "I told him."

"But..." What was he saying? Dara bit her lower lip. If her grandfather knew, no way would he have let her out of his sight unless... "No." She stared at the man beside her. "No!"

"I'm afraid so, sweetheart." He sounded sorry, but all he looked was eager—eager to get this over with.

"It's not as if you were madly in love with me or anything," he argued. "You just want to stick it to your grandfather."

"That's not true!" At least part of it wasn't true.

He looked skeptical. "Regardless of that, you can't deny there *is* a bright side."

"I can't imagine what it might be!"

"Simply this. We'd never have stuck it out for the five years it'd take us to get control of your trust fund, and if we divorced, we'd have lost everything."

"How did you know about my...?" She gasped. "Grandfather told you."

"How I know isn't important. What's important is that we'd never be able to stay together until you turn thirty and we both know it."

"I *don't* know it!" Dara clenched her hands until her nails cut into her palms. "At least, I didn't. Blake, you said you loved me." Of course, she'd said she loved him, too, when in fact she was doubtful that soul-deep, romantic love, the kind in books and movies, actually existed. She'd simply decided to settle for what she could get.

Which apparently did not include Blake.

"Yeah, I do love you," he said, "but frankly, I love money more. That's the way it works out here in the real world as opposed to that ivory tower you've always lived in. I can take my cut now and it's a sure thing. Or I can try to stick it out for five years and in the process make us both miserable."

She pressed palms, cool and trembling, flat against her burning cheeks. "I risked everything for you,

Blake,'' she blurted, ''my self-respect, even my financial future. How can you humiliate me like this?''

''Because, in my own way, I really do care for you…and because your grandfather's made me a remarkably generous offer. In fact, it's an offer I can't refuse.'' He patted her knee, his movements uncharacteristically awkward. ''A little humiliation now is better than a lot of humiliation later,'' he said in a coaxing tone. ''Once you're over the shock, you'll see I'm right.''

''All I'll see is that you're—you're as bad as my grandfather said you were!''

''Sticks and stones. Give it up, Dara. As long as big bucks are involved, you're never going to get away from Donald Linnell.'' He squared his shoulders. ''Can I drop you off at the hotel? I've got a plane to catch so I don't have a lot of time.''

''No!'' She fumbled for the door latch. How could she possibly have been fooled by this worm? ''I'd rather walk all the way back to California than spend another minute in your company.''

He looked pained. ''That's a rather childish attitude, but suit yourself.''

''I intend to.'' Dara threw open the door. Holding it wide, she stared at him with that jarring, red neon glow on his face. Finally, she saw him for the devil he was.

He said with unusual seriousness, ''Someday you'll see I'm right and thank me.''

Her pride came to her rescue. ''I'm thanking you now.''

But it was bravado. Watching the automobile pull

away from the curb, she blinked back tears even as she lifted her chin defiantly. Would she never find a man strong enough to withstand the blandishments of her grandfather? She wasn't asking for the impossible. She didn't expect *great love,* the kind the poets sang about.

Infatuation she had known; she'd been infatuated with Blake once upon a time. Even so, she'd have been a good wife to him—she would! She had worked hard to convince herself that mutual respect and consideration would be enough to build a good marriage.

Now all she felt was defeat and humiliation. Of *course,* she was better off without him, she knew that now. But his betrayal still hurt.

"Excuse me, little lady, but are you lost or somethin'?"

She started, whirling to face the man who'd spoken. One of the ebb and flow of humanity milling about on the sidewalk, he was an old guy dressed like a cowboy: jeans and boots and a long-sleeved plaid shirt. An enormous shiny buckle anchored his broad leather belt, and the hat shoved back on his grizzled head had seen better days. When he smiled, deep creases appeared in his leathery face.

Dara met his concerned gaze. "Thank you, but I'm not lost," she said stiffly.

"I dunno." He shoved the hat farther back with one thumb. "You're about the lostest-lookin' little thing I've seen in a coon's age." Only he didn't exactly say *thing;* he said *thang.*

She found herself smiling back at him even through all the confusion and hurt. She was glad to have even this small distraction. "I just need a telephone," she said. "Would you happen to know where I could find one?"

"Sure thang." He indicated the dazzling facade in front of which they were standing: the words "The Golden Gringo" and an animated figure of a cowboy on a bucking horse glowed with electric power. "C'mon in and I'll point you to it."

He seemed harmless enough, but Dara wasn't in the habit of following strangers anywhere, especially into bars. "I don't know...." She edged away. "I think what I really need is a cab. Maybe if I just stand here—"

"Howdy, sweet thang!" The words emanated from a group of much younger cowboys passing by. One of them brushed against Dara, then leaped back, sweeping his white hat from unruly hair. "Can I buy you a drink, good-lookin'?"

"She's with me, cowboy." The old man fixed the younger one with a withering scowl.

The young one took a step back, finally dragging his gaze from Dara to the speaker. He did a double take. "Well, howdy, Slim. Didn't know this was a friend of the Bar F."

"Now you do," the man called Slim said with a friendly smile that got serious around the edges. "Why don't you boys run along and stop botherin' ladies."

"We'll do that." The cowboy doffed his hat again, this time respectfully. "Beg pardon, ma'am. Beg pardon." He practically bowed himself away.

Dara hadn't needed saving, but it had been done so nicely that she smiled at her "rescuer". "Slim, is it?"

He nodded. "Slim Sanders, ma'am, of the Bar F Ranch in Faraway, Colorado."

"Colorado *is* far away," she agreed, working on hearsay; she'd never been there or even thought much about the state, so she had only the vaguest sense of its location.

He grinned. "Yes, but that ain't what I meant. The name of the *town* is Faraway. It's up in the mountains west a Denver. But that ain't neither here nor there." He took her elbow and she didn't object. "You just come on in here with me and I'll see you're taken care of. Not a thang to worry about. I'll look out for you, little lady. You might even call this a family-type establishment, at least durin' the NFR every December."

She let him lead her forward. At least he was taking her mind off her problems, however briefly. "What's an NFR?" she asked.

"You don't know what the NFR is? Why, little lady, that's the National Finals Rodeo and it's the biggest thang goin', includin' that so-called Super Bowl and the World Serious…"

Still talking, he opened the door and steered her into the bedlam inside.

And inside, she'd met a handsome cowboy named Zane Farley, a man who looked at her now with such sympathetic understanding that to her vast dismay, she felt a tear begin its silent slide down her cheek.

CHAPTER TWO

ZANE couldn't believe it. First Jody and now this pretty little piece of calico. Didn't women ever think about anything except getting married? Made a man wonder....

But not enough to keep him from doing what came naturally. Slipping his arms around Dara's slender shoulders, he held her gently against his chest. There was nothing personal in it, he told himself, just one human being offering comfort to another.

She melted against him with a sigh, as if she'd longed for such solace. Sliding her arms around his waist, she clung to him.

Holding her like that, he couldn't imagine how any man could pull such a damned cowardly trick. Hell, it defied reason! "You're better off without that idiot," he muttered against her pale hair, even softer against his cheek than he'd imagined it would be.

"I know." She seemed to gather herself, then straightened away from him as if struck by a sudden attack of shyness. She cleared her throat. "Or at least I'll know it soon. Right now, it still...hurts."

"I reckon it would." He wished she hadn't pulled away from his embrace. He'd enjoyed the feel of her body against his, at once firm and soft. In addition, her sudden movement had made him...dizzy? He blinked and looked around, realizing the room had become hazy and sort of out of focus. He shook his head and blinked again, but his vision didn't clear.

He wondered hazily what was in that pill he'd downed. Was it reacting with the alcohol? Maybe he should cut off the beer. Maybe he should head back to the motel. Maybe he should—

"Hey, ol' buddy, who you got there?"

A whole pack of cowboys converged on them, their attention on Dara, a new face, and a beautiful one at that. Zane tried to discourage them with a threatening scowl. "Nobody! Isn't it time you fellas headed back to the motel? Tomorrow's a big day."

"Got plenty of time. Beertender, bring us some bars!"

"Naw, I mean it," Zane insisted. "Me'n' this lady have things to talk about."

"What things?"

"Important things. She needs…" He was having trouble concentrating. "Hell, she needs advice."

"I know how to give advice," the short cowboy at the back of the pack, the one who'd given Zane the pills earlier, hollered. "I give the best advice in Cheyenne, Wyoming."

"I got you beat in Provo, Utah," another chimed in. "Once I get started, I don't know when to stop. Just tell me your troubles, darlin', because I am here to help!"

And that's how Zane and Dara and Slim ended up at a big round table in the corner, drinking beer and eating popcorn out of paper napkin–lined plastic baskets and listening to the "advice" of a half-dozen half-sober cowpokes.

*　　*　　*

Dara had never been around people like these, down-to-earth people who apparently said exactly what they thought without prevarication and said it with a great good humor that enchanted her. She found herself responding…slowly at first, and then when her comments met with nothing but the greatest of respect and attention, with more confidence.

Finally, one of the cowboys asked the inevitable. "How'd a nice city girl like you wind up in a country place like the Golden Gringo?"

Once again, she resorted to the truth. With good-looking Zane Farley sitting beside her, Blake Williams already seemed to have receded into no more than a bitter memory.

So she said, "I was just dumped on my way to a wedding chapel by a man more interested in my grandfather's money than in me."

"No!" They stared at her in mutual horror!

She basked in their astonishment. "It's not the first time, either," she confided. "My grandfather is not only wealthy, he's also very…bossy."

The short cowboy shook his head in disbelief. "No self-respectin' man would do such a thing," he declared to the general agreement of his peers. "Sure hope he didn't go and break your heart or nothin'."

Dara considered. Blake had hurt her feelings, no doubt about that, but the effect the silently observing Zane had on her in no way supported a broken-heart theory. "I'll get over him," she said at last. "But what about the next time—and the next? I may never find a man capable of standing up to my grandfather."

"Nah! No need to worry about that! A nice-lookin' gal like you?"

"Everybody's got their price, apparently." She spoke the sad truth as she knew it. "Grandfather pulls out his checkbook and I don't stand a chance."

"Somebody oughta take your granddaddy down a peg or two," a broad-shouldered man who'd been introduced as a bulldogger declared. This pronouncement met with a general murmur of agreement.

"I thought I'd found the man who would," Dara said with a defeated sigh, "and look where it got me. No, I might as well give up. Blake Williams was my very last chance and now I—"

"That man was a fool. He wasn't worthy of you."

At Zane's emphatic statement, Dara blinked and cocked her head to look at him. His dark eyes were half-closed as if he could almost *see* the object of his scorn. His strong jaw was set in a stern line.

"Thanks for your vote of support," she said uncertainly, "but—"

"Hell," he interrupted, shifting in his chair so he could meet her puzzled gaze, "you don't need that guy. Somebody'll marry you one of these days and take you away from your big bad granddaddy." He took a deep breath, his already broad chest expanding. "I've got half a mind to marry you myself!"

The table erupted in a general outpouring of surprise, quickly followed by approval. For her part, Dara simply stared. Then it occurred to her that he was joking.

She laughed weakly, but the thought of *this man* as *husband* sent a sharp jolt of excitement singing through her veins. "Very funny," she said. "If Grandfather was upset about an actor, I can just imagine how he'd feel about a cowboy."

Zane leaned forward, pushing his empty beer glass aside. His gaze burned into her. "I had no intention of bein' funny," he said in a steely tone. "Nor do I give two hoots in hell how your granddaddy feels about it. How do *you* feel?"

"Why, I—it's not—I can't…" But even while she stammered over a response, she knew how she felt. Excited. Scared. And sorry that she hadn't met this man under circumstances more conducive to *real* romance. He wiped out memories of every other man she'd ever known, including the one who'd just tap-danced all over her self-esteem. The chemistry between them was so powerful that she couldn't even *talk*.

"Hot damn!" The short cowboy banged a hand flat on the table, making the assortment of beer bottles dance. "That's just what we need to liven up these proceedings, folks—a weddin'!"

Slim stood up, looking alarmed. Planting his palms on the table, he leaned forward to gain the spotlight. "You people are crazy as pet coons," he declared, his pale blue eyes snapping. "These two folks cain't get married. Hell, they only met two hours ago."

"So what?" Shorty challenged. "How long'd you know that *Blake* fella, Dara?"

She thought. "About six months."

"And it's plain as the nose on your face that you didn't *really* know him, am I right? He led you down the garden path, am I right? So it don't really matter how long you know somebody if they're the wrong somebody. If they're the right somebody, it can hit you fast as—fast as greased lightnin'." Looking well satisfied with himself, he leaned back in his chair and crossed his arms over his chest as if daring anyone to disagree with him.

A moment of universal silence met his pronouncement and then the table erupted in a buzz of approval. Even Dara found herself grinning. Only Slim seemed unmoved.

"Zane Farley," the old cowboy grumbled, "you know you got no intention in the world of gettin' married. Why, you're the one always said no woman would ever rope and hog-tie *you*."

"That's just it!" Zane's smile looked triumphant. "She didn't even *try*. This is all my idea, not hers. It's when women come after me with the hobbles already in their hands that I start running backward."

"But—"

Dara found her voice at last. "Relax, Slim. I'm not going to put Zane's sincerity to the test."

Zane looked affronted. "You saying I'm not sincere?"

"Not at all." Meeting his offended gaze, she felt herself softening toward him even more. He really was the most powerfully attractive man she'd ever met. Unfortunately, that didn't change the facts. "You're just doing the gallant, gracious...idiotic thing—no, don't be offended!" she added when he tried to interrupt. "Let *me* do the decent thing by letting you off the hook with my gratitude."

"Now, Dara..." He caught one of her hands between his and stroked it. "I'm proposing marriage and I'll stand by it till hell freezes over."

"Because you feel sorry for me." She shook her head with a sigh, trying to ignore the pleasures of his touch. "That's not enough, but I do appreciate the gesture." She pulled her hand from his although she didn't want to, then stood up. "I think I'd better be going before I weaken." She glanced around the table. "You've all been wonderful to me and—"

A chorus of disclaimers erupted. Shorty yelled, "Why don't you court her, Zane? She don't know yet how charmin' you can be when you put your mind to it!"

She didn't even want to *think* about trying to resist Zane if he ever really put her resolve to the test. She managed a shaky smile, feeling suddenly very alone. "Call me old-fashioned, but this *is* a trifle fast. We know nothing about each other."

"I know all about *you*," Zane said triumphantly. "Your granddaddy's rich and bossy and he's played hell with your love life."

"That's hardly the whole story."

"I know you're what my pa used to call pretty as a little speckled pup. That's gotta count for something."

Laughing at what seemed to her like a backhanded compliment, she still felt a flush of pleasure. "Thanks, but that's not quite enough to base a lifetime of togetherness on."

"I know you're nice," he plunged ahead. "You're also flexible—you fit right in with my rowdy friends."

"Thanks again."

"You're brave and I respect that. You feel like cryin', but you don't."

His unexpected sensitivity brought a lump to her throat, but she refused to shed tears for her own stupidity when he'd just complimented her. It was time to lighten the mood. "Okay, I'll concede you know me like a book," she teased, her voice husky. "But I don't know you at all."

Shorty let out a whoop. "I'll vouch for him," he hollered. "Good family, owns a nice spread in the Colorado mountains. Acourse, Zane here spends mosta his time followin' the circuit, so—"

"Circuit?" She had no idea what that meant.

Shorty nodded. "Rodeo circuit." He indicated the others at the table. "That's what we all do, except for old Slim, acourse."

"Rodeo." She said it like a foreign word. She'd never seen a rodeo in her life, or wanted to. She cast a sideways glance at Zane. "What is it you do in the rodeo?"

He seemed to pull himself together with an effort. His eyes looked a little glazed, probably with exhaustion. "I rope calves and wrestle...wrestle steers mostly."

"You *wrestle* steers? Those great big cows?" She stared at him, shocked.

He choked. His friends burst into great guffaws. He picked up Slim's glass of beer and downed it. Slim sat down in disgust and crossed his arms over his chest.

"Steers and cows," Zane announced, "are two entirely different critters. But we won't go into that just yet. Don't want to scare you off if I can help it." He cast a baleful glance around the table as if daring his friends to disagree.

Shorty piped up. "You never hearda Zane Farley? He's just been world champion four times is all."

She was impressed. "Really? But that just proves my point. I'm ignorant. We can't get married. Common sense is against it."

"But maybe fate's for it," Slim inserted suddenly.

Zane gave his friend a puzzled look. "I thought you were against this."

"I was, but maybe I changed my mind. Acourse, she's clearly too good for you."

Zane nodded. "I'll give you that, but whaddaya mean, *fate?*"

"Fate's what brung you two together. You can't fight fate. If you just gotta try, I can guaran-danged-tee you it ain't gonna work."

This was getting too deep for Dara. "Let's leave fate out of it, okay?" She smiled impersonally at the lot of them. "It's late and I've got to be going. But I want to thank all of you for cheering me up. Blake Williams obviously wasn't the man for me. Right now, I'm feeling almost...lucky I found it out in time."

"That ain't luck," Slim declared with complete certainty. "It's fate."

"Whatever." She pushed back her chair and rose.

Zane looked at her through narrowed eyes, long lashes casting shadows on his high cheekbones. "You

sure you don't want to get married?'' he asked plaintively.

She bit her bottom lip, forcing herself to say the
right thing. ''I'm sure. But thanks anyway.''

Slim dug around in his jeans pocket. ''Will you do
me one little favor before you go?'' he asked suddenly, a crafty gleam in his eye.

A warning bell went off in her mind, but still she
said, ''If I can.''

He held out his hand. ''Take this quarter over to
that there slot machine and give 'er a pull for me.''

She took the coin and looked down at it nestled in
her palm. ''Okay, but I don't get it.''

''I do!'' Shorty yelled. ''Fate!''

The entire table rose to troop behind her to the slot
machine—all except Zane, that is. Once there, she
looked at the assortment of bars and cherries,
shrugged and dropped in the coin. Pulling the handle,
she watched the icons begin their spin without interest.

Slim might believe fate could be found in the spin
of a slot machine, but she didn't. Slipping through the
crowd, she returned to the table and Zane. Touching
his shoulder lightly to get his attention, she felt the
strangely exciting zap of electricity again and quickly
dropped her hand.

He started as if he felt it, too, and looked up with
a question in his eyes. Tousled dark hair spilled over
his forehead and intriguing shadows softened the an-
gles of his lean face.

''Thank you for everything,'' she said softly. ''You
and your friends have helped me through a very dif-

ficult time. If we had met under other circumstances—''

A wave of excitement erupted from the circle of
those same friends clustered around the slot machine.
But their voices couldn't mask the clashing sound of
coins banging into the metal receptacle. Zane and
Dara stared at each other.

''Jackpot!'' somebody yelled.

''Fate!'' Zane murmured.

Everybody agreed that the jackpot, which Dara insisted Slim keep, was a sign: Dara and Zane were
obviously lucky for each other.

Exhausted both physically and mentally, caught in
some almost mystical zone, Dara found herself almost
inclined to agree. In fact, she found herself joining in
the general jubilation.

Slim and several other cowboys slammed numerous
plastic cups of quarters down on the table. ''Did I tell
you or what?'' he demanded of Zane. ''It's a sign.''
He cast a glance heavenward before going on. ''You
two kids are meant for each other. It's fate, I tell you,
fate!''

''Yeah, fate!'' Shorty pounded Zane on the back.
''Ask her again, cowboy! Maybe you'll get lucky!''

Zane stood up. Taking Dara's hands in his, he drew
her forward. She could hardly breathe; she certainly
couldn't resist. When they stood facing each other,
gazes locked, he spoke. ''Will I get lucky this time,
Dara?''

She licked her lips but couldn't pull her gaze away.

Her hands trembled in his. "I...don't know. I'm really confused...."

"I'm confused, too," he agreed, his voice soft and his expression tender. "Nothing like this has ever happened to me before, either."

Maybe he did understand. She gave him a tremulous smile. "Are we crazy?"

"That depends." The crooked little grin on his face made her heart lurch. "Are you about to say yes?"

"I can't know that until I'm asked a question."

"Then here's the question. Dara...sweetheart, what do you say? Want to get married?"

She sensed the collective holding of breath of those surrounding them and waiting for her answer, but she didn't let that intimidate her. She drew a deep breath. "Guess this proves it," she said in a strong, clear voice. "We *are* crazy—because my answer is yes!"

With a whoop that vibrated with jubilation, he grabbed her in a wild embrace and kissed her. Even in the midst of bedlam, she lost herself in the brief joy of his mouth on hers. The feel of his strong arms added to the tumult of emotions shooting through her. *What's happening to me?* she wondered. *What's this man doing to me?*

He held her away to look into her face and she saw that he was breathing hard. He was also smiling broadly, but his eyes still held that almost glazed sheen, as if he was lost in the same fantasy world that claimed her.

"Do you mean it?" he asked.

She licked her lips nervously and appealed to the

crowd around them. "If your friends will vouch for your good character."

They roared with laughter and applause and then Shorty spoke for all of them. "Don't know about good character, but he's never been in jail that I know of and he don't beat his horses," he declared. "He comes from good folks. Acourse, if you marry him, it'll break a lot of female hearts, includin' a certain little barrel—"

"Hush up," Slim blustered. He frowned at Dara and Zane. "You kids really gonna tie the knot?"

Zane hugged Dara tight against his side. "Looks like it."

"When?"

Zane's brows rose. "There's no time like the present. Hell, we're in Las Vegas. Let's do it!"

"Let's do it!" Dara agreed, but her heart seemed to stop beating. It was an outlandish proposal. She could hardly believe she was about to grab for the ring on the merry-go-round she'd been riding almost since she got the braces off her teeth. Would that ring turn out to be gold or brass?

Dara Linnell and Zane Farley exchanged marriage vows at the Many Happy Returns Chapel in Las Vegas only hours after meeting. "Faster than greased lightning," Shorty said admiringly.

Shorty was one of the witnesses; Slim was the other. But they were by no means the only guests. Almost the entire crowd from the Golden Gringo went along.

Dara had had a bad moment at the license bureau

when one of the clerks did a double take and said, "You back? What happened to the other guy?"

Zane had come to her rescue. "She fell in love with me and dumped him," he drawled. "Now get a move on because we gotta make up for lost time."

After the ceremony, the gang of cowboys escorted the newlyweds to Dara's suite at the MGM Grand Hotel, where she called for champagne. After kisses for the bride and toasts to the happy couple, the cowboys bowed out with many sly glances and wishes for happiness. Finally, everyone was gone except Slim, who shook hands with the bridegroom but didn't offer to leave.

Shrugging, Zane disappeared into the bedroom. When he was gone, Slim grimaced. "I hope I done right," he said in his gravelly voice.

Fighting her nervousness, Dara tried to reassure him. "This was my choice," she said bravely. "No matter how it turns out, I'll never blame you—or anyone."

He sighed. "You're a fine gal, Dara...Farley, it is now."

Dara Farley! She felt almost faint with the realization of what she'd just done. "T-thank you," she managed to murmur.

"He's a good boy, too."

She glanced toward the closed door behind which her new husband waited. "I'm sure—I hope so." She wasn't actually sure of anything except that no man had ever affected her the way Zane did. Was that enough upon which to build a future? Okay, it would doubtless turn out to be infatuation, not love—infatuation at first sight—but if they both tried really hard, they could build something good. She was sure of it.

"Your granddaddy will never back that boy down," Slim predicted. "You don't have to worry about that part anymore."

"That's a relief." She hadn't thought of her grandfather for hours. Or Blake, either. All she could think about was Zane and the enormous leap of faith she'd just made.

Together she and Slim walked toward the hall door in a niche between the bedroom and the sitting room. There he turned, his grizzled face troubled.

"I don't know what come over him to do what he done," Slim said very seriously, "but it's what he needs. It's what every man needs—the love of a good woman. The boy's twenty-nine and he's been tomcattin' around way too long." He brightened. "But that's over now. He's got him the prettiest little wife anybody ever saw and that's a fact." Leaning forward, he kissed her on the cheek. "Be good to each other," he advised.

She smiled, thinking it would be easy to be good to Zane Farley. "Fate," she reminded Slim with a smile.

He chuckled. "Yeah, and it just keeps on happenin', don't it?" Shaking his grizzled head, he opened the door and was gone.

For a moment, Dara stood there undecided. Suddenly, she, too, wanted to open the door and just run. But she couldn't do that—she didn't *really* want to do that. She was nervous, that was all. All brides were, weren't they?

She looked longingly at a half-empty bottle of champagne in the silver cooler but didn't succumb to the lure of false courage. She'd never had a wedding night before and she wanted to remember every detail....

CHAPTER THREE

ZANE was having a helluva time prying his eyelids open.

He lay on his back on something soft—a mattress? If it was, it didn't feel like the one in the motel room he'd been sharing with Slim not far from the Thomas and Mack Center, Las Vegas site of the National Finals Rodeo.

His mouth felt as if a herd of buffalo had recently stampeded through it. Even with his eyes closed, his head spun in woozy circles and his stomach clenched into a mass of muscle.

What the hell had happened last night?

Calm down, he told himself. Take it slowly and rationally.

He remembered going to the Golden Gringo with his friends. He remembered that he'd been hurting from previous encounters with large bovine creatures and he remembered having a couple of beers and then somebody—he *didn't* remember who—had offered him a pain pill, which he refused. About then, Slim had walked in with a good-looking blonde and Zane, like a damn fool, had held out his hand for God-only-knew what kind of prescription drug.

He groaned. He knew he shouldn't have taken somebody else's prescription medication. He knew pain pills and alcohol didn't mix and he'd already had a couple of beers. But had that stopped him?

He'd taken the pill and that was virtually the last memory he had of a night that must have gone on far too long, judging by the way he felt. He hoped he hadn't made a total jackass out of himself. And if that was too much to hope for, he hoped nobody had seen him do it.

In addition to a throbbing head, he realized his cramped muscles were screaming for relief. Cautiously, he tried to shift his position but found he couldn't; something warm and soft seemed to be pinning down his entire left side and arm, while every other part of him was icy cold. The soft *whoosh* of the air conditioner penetrated his foggy brain and he frowned and tried to think.

When he'd left this room yesterday morning, the air conditioner had been roaring like a jet plane although it wasn't putting out enough cold air to chill an overheated imagination. In fact, he'd complained to the clerk on the way out. Obviously, somebody had fixed it while he was gone. Otherwise he wouldn't be freezing his patootie off.

With superhuman effort, he forced his eyes open just a crack. Since he was lying on his back, all he saw was the opposite side of the room, where the wall met the ceiling. It was a pale, creamy beige, as smooth and clean as a fresh sheet of paper.

The room he remembered had been accented by tired orange-and-brown-striped walls.

This was not that room.

Where the hell was he?

He heard a soft sound—a sigh?—and every muscle in his body tightened with alarm. He was not alone. With growing consternation, he confronted a new dilemma fighting its way into his wobbly thoughts.

Who the hell was in this bed with him?

Dara sighed again and snuggled closer to the warm body beside hers, reluctant to leave the safe cocoon of sleep. Only half-awake, she let her mind wander over the events of the previous evening and all that had followed. It hadn't exactly been the wedding or the wedding night of her dreams, she concluded, but they had all the time in the world....

Last night when she'd entered the bedroom of her suite, she'd found her handsome cowboy sprawled naked on the bed, sound asleep. For a long time, she'd just stood there admiring the long, tapered muscles of his back and shoulders, the narrow waist and hips before they disappeared beneath the silky sheet. His dark hair lay tousled on the pillow, giving him the endearing look of a little boy.

But he wasn't a little boy. He was a magnificent specimen of manhood...and her husband. Would he regret that fact when he awakened? She prayed not with all her heart because...he was already more to her than just a way out from beneath her grandfather's domination. Much more.

Dara Linnell was not a woman who believed in love at first sight—or second sight or tenth—yet she was already at least half-convinced she could love this stranger. She just needed to learn a few more details about him—little things like when he was born, whether he had a family, minor stuff like that. Once they got to know each other better, any lingering reservations would evaporate.

Preparing for bed, she'd thought about the way fate—Slim was right; it *was* fate!—had brought them together. She knew the obstacles they'd face and that it wouldn't be easy. She also knew she had a reputation for giving up when the going got tough, but this time she just knew she'd done the right thing.

Her grandfather would never intimidate this cowboy! Wearing the filmy white gown she'd chosen for a wedding night with another man, she'd turned off the light and crept self-consciously into bed beside Zane.

He'd made a strangled sound deep in his chest and rolled over onto his side to face her. Grateful for the opportunity, she'd slipped beneath one extended arm, resting her weary head on his smooth, strong shoulder.

Married! She'd whispered the word aloud to herself. She was married....

But now a new day had dawned and she wasn't sure she was ready to wake up from all those pleasant thoughts and dreams. What would happen when she opened her eyes? Would he be smiling at her, waiting to tell her how sorry he was that he'd fallen asleep waiting for her to join him in bed? Would he be worried that she'd be angry or even that she wouldn't forgive him? Would he be sorry that their first night as husband and wife had been spent...sleeping?

An indulgent smile tugged at her lips. She would assure him that she understood! He'd been doing whatever rodeo cowboys did all day, which apparently was hard and dangerous work, although precisely what that entailed remained a mystery to her. No wonder he'd been exhausted. She must assure him that she'd be an understanding wife.

Smiling, she opened her eyes slowly, languorously—and found him watching her. His eyes looked bloodshot and angry. She caught her breath in confusion.

And then he asked in rapid succession, "What time is it? Where am I?" and the topper, *"Who the hell are you?"*

She felt her face freeze, wiping away the smile with which she'd greeted him. He hoisted himself on an elbow, bouncing her off his arm in the process.

Through it all, he just kept glaring at her.

She swallowed hard. "W-why...*Dara* and you darn well know it." Spunk returning, she frowned at him, thoroughly confused by his attitude.

"Dara." He rolled his eyes. "Dara what?"

She gasped. "Dara Farley!"

That stopped him cold. His eyes widened in shock. *"Farley?* Are we...related in some way that escapes me?"

She sat up abruptly, which gave her a better view of his long, lean body. Only a corner of the sheet barely covered his most personal aspects. "You could say we're related," she yelled at him, "if *married* counts!"

He went absolutely, totally, completely still. An expression of horror suffused his face. "Married. As in..." With a trembling hand, he indicated first her, then himself. ''...you and me?'' He looked on the verge of passing out.

''Darn you, Zane!'' She felt hot tears burn her eyes and dashed the moisture away with one hand. ''Don't try to tell me you don't remember!''

''I don't,'' he said flatly.

She didn't—*couldn't*—believe him. ''You don't remember me hitting the jackpot at the Golden Gringo and Slim saying it was fate?''

''Slim was there?''

''Yes, and Shorty and a lot of other cowboys.''

He looked stricken. ''Great. Witnesses!'' He sucked in a ragged breath. ''What the hell does you hitting a jackpot have to do with...?'' He looked around wildly, swallowing convulsively.

''Everything! Once I hit the jackpot, they all agreed—including you—that we were lucky for each other. So everybody went with us to get the marriage license and then we went to a wedding chapel and then everybody brought us back here—''

''Where's *here?*''

''The MGM Grand. I suppose you're going to tell me you don't remember carrying me down the yellow brick road?''

''Why would I do that? You told me your name was Dara, not Dorothy.''

''Ohhh!'' She clenched her hands into impotent fists. ''And I thought you were a gentleman!''

''Did you?'' He looked grim. ''Have I always been...was I...uh...a gentleman last night?''

''When we got married? Of course! Do you think I'd have married a—a hoodlum?''

"I don't know what you'd marry." He licked his lips uneasily. "I don't know a thing about you. What I'm trying to ask is…uh…then what happened?"

"I told you," she said patiently. "Then everybody came to my suite and had champagne and then they all left and we went to bed and I don't believe for a single minute that you've forgotten!"

He looked sick. Dropping back on the bed, he covered his face with his hands and groaned. "What floor is this room on?" he asked suddenly.

"I don't know. Third, maybe? Why do you want to know?"

"Because I'm thinking about jumping out of the window and I want to be sure the fall will kill me."

"We don't have a window!" She wasn't sure that was true but didn't want him looking around for one. "Zane Farley, how can you—"

A pounding on the outside door interrupted her, but only momentarily.

"Treat me this way after I was completely honest with you? You said—"

The pounding accelerated and Zane pressed his palms against his temples and shuddered as if the blows were striking him instead of the door.

"That you understood and that you'd—"

"Dara!" The single word roared through the heavy hotel door, followed by, "Dara Linnell, you open this door! Hotel management's right behind me and if you don't do as I say, they'll open it for you!"

Dara let out a little shriek of horror. "My God," she cried, throwing herself against Zane's chest and clutching at his shoulders with all her strength. "It's my grandfather! What are we going to do?"

The door to the bedroom flew open. Instinctively, Zane tightened his arms around the trembling shoulders of—his bride? Was he really married to this woman? Had he already asserted his marital rights and just didn't remember?

Son of a—

A man charged into the room, breathing fire. Of medium height, he seemed considerably larger in his fury. Silver hair, matching a silver mustache, swept away from his temples. His fiery blue eyes somehow managed to appear hot and cold at the same time. Although of advanced years, he looked and moved like a much younger man.

His gaze zeroed in to the couple on the bed and he started forward, hands clenching. "I'll thank you to take your hands off my granddaughter!" he shouted.

Zane sat up, deliberately keeping Dara on his lap. She continued to cling to him, her face pressed against his bare shoulder. "Are you talking about my *wife?*" he challenged the outraged man.

The intruder stopped short, a succession of emotions passing across his face, which finally settled into lines of disbelief. "You two are married?" he choked.

Zane felt Dara draw a great shuddering breath. Then with what seemed an enormous effort, she straightened. Without releasing her hold on him, she looked over her shoulder.

"We were married last night," she said in a voice that trembled with bravado. "Or maybe it was this morning.... Anyway, I'm Mrs. Zane Farley and there's nothing you can do about it, Grandfather.''

"The hell there's not!" The man thrust a hand through his neat hair, leaving it disheveled. "I need a drink." He glanced around the room. "I'd settle for coffee."

"I'm sorry," Dara said. "We just woke up and there hasn't been time—"

"I don't want to hear that kind of talk," the man roared. Striding to the telephone on a table, he yanked up the receiver and shouted at room service. Turning back to the couple still on the bed, he hesitated for a moment with his hands clenching and opening while he tried to regain control of himself.

Dara licked her lips, which Zane belatedly noticed were really quite delectable. "Uh...Grandfather, I'd like you to meet my husband, Zane Farley. Z-Zane—darling, this is my grandfather, Donald Linnell."

Zane said, "Howdy," wondering how he was going to get out of *this* jam. He should just speak up, explain that he really didn't remember any of this and promise that he'd be out of both their lives at the earliest opportunity. But something stopped him even before the man answered.

"Howdy." Linnell gave it back with a generous helping of sarcasm. "Now that the niceties are out of the way, would you two like to get up and put some clothes on? This is not the kind of scene a grandfather likes walking in on."

"Oh!" Dara looked down at herself helplessly; Zane looked down at her, too.

The true extent of her vulnerability struck him right in the solar plexus, quickly followed by the realization that she was gorgeous. She sat there with that cloud of curly blond hair brushing her shoulders and sleep-softened face, and long, curving lashes framing slightly slanting green eyes. Her skin looked like fine satin, but the expression on her oval face was one of such insecurity that Zane found his resentments melting away.

Then he realized how little her nightgown left to the imagination despite a profusion of lace and ribbons. White and semisheer, the top cut deeply between thrusting breasts while the skirt pooled around her hips, baring slim and shapely legs below the knee.

How could he have slept with her and not even remember? He knew he'd never forget her *now,* not after seeing her like this.

She scrambled from the bed as if finally deciding upon the best course of action. "I have a robe," she said brightly, picking up another bit of froth from the bench at the foot of the bed. Slipping into it, she smiled uncertainly at her grandfather. "Is that better?"

Linnell groaned. "Not much, but I don't suppose I should worry about locking the barn door after— never mind that. You…"

He turned his disapproval on Zane, who slid to the edge of the bed and stood, tugging the sheet with him. He was naked, which was how he usually slept. But in this instance, he had no idea in the world where his clothing might be.

It took some effort, but eventually the sheet slid

free of the mattress and he wrapped it snugly around his hips. Turning, he found Dara staring at him. This annoyed him. He wasn't the one in trouble; she was. He tucked one corner of the sheet in at the waist and gave his presumed grandfather-in-law a level, challenging stare. "You got the time?"

The older man blinked. "Time for what?"

"The time." Zane pointed at the heavy gold watch on the man's wrist.

"Oh, that time." Linnell checked. "It's going on nine. Now I want one of you to tell me—"

"Nine!" Zane's stomach muscles clenched. "I'm supposed to meet some people at the arena at—"

"Forget it. One of you has got to tell me what the hell is going on here!" Linnell swung on his granddaughter, who shrank back. "Dara, you owe me an explanation. How did this happen? What are you trying to prove? That you can find a fortune hunter under every rock? Or did you get him drunk and—"

"Now just a doggone minute!" Zane clenched his jaw and his hands; this was getting way too personal. The sheet drooped precariously and he fumbled it back into place.

Dara made a little sound of protest and both men turned their irate glances upon her. She hesitated, chewing on her lip. Then she sighed.

"All right," she said in a voice that trembled. "I'll tell you everything—"

Before she could go on, a knock on the door announced the arrival of coffee. While the bellman wheeled in the cart, Zane darted into the bathroom, where he was relieved to find the clothes he'd worn to the Golden Gringo last night in a heap in one corner of the spacious room. Dragging on his Wrangler jeans, he trotted back out barefooted, bare chested and loaded for bear.

If Dara was going to explain what had happened, he sure as hell didn't want to miss hearing it! When he entered the sitting room, Dara looked up from the coffee service with an uncertain smile. "Coffee, dear?"

"Yeah," Zane growled, "and don't..." He'd been about to say *and don't call me dear* but changed that to "mess with it. I take mine straight."

She looked relieved. "Of course." She served him.

Linnell turned away from the window, his movements sharp and edgy. "Quit stalling, Dara, and tell me how this happened. I thought I had everything all taken care of."

She sat in an easy chair, holding her cup and saucer primly on her knee. The light caught on the stone of the ring on her right hand. From the flash, Zane knew it was a diamond. No rings on her left hand, though.

She spoke in a small, tired voice. "You took care of Blake anyway. How much did it cost you to buy him off, Grandfather?"

Linnell shrugged. "Less than some of the others. So did you have a replacement standing by just in case or—" he indicated Zane with a careless toss of one hand "—was your meeting with this fellow unfortunate happenstance?"

Damn! Out of the blue, Zane remembered where he'd seen her! She'd walked into the Golden Gringo with Slim just before those damned pills went down his gullet. He appreciated the memory because it put him into a better position to protect her.

"We met in a bar," he said in a "doesn't everybody?" tone. "I picked her up. Wanna make something of it?"

Linnell recoiled; Dara didn't.

"We may as well tell the truth," she said. "*I* picked *him* up, Grandfather. It…was just one of those things. What can I say? Perhaps it was fate."

Fate! From somewhere, another memory surfaced in Zane's muddled brain of Slim and the others saying that word over and over again. Zane strained to remember, finally flashing on the bedlam in the bar, on himself saying something stupid about…about *getting married*…and Dara…

The details eluded him, so he said, "I guess fate's as good an explanation as any. Yeah, we'll call it fate."

"Or terminal stupidity." Linnell glared at his granddaughter, who squared her shoulders and lifted her chin defiantly before the disapproval in his gaze.

Zane always admired spirit. He crossed the room and rested one hand lightly on her shoulder. She looked up with surprise on her lovely face. That expression was quickly replaced by gratitude, which made him feel uneasy.

Nevertheless, he returned her smile. "Look," he said, "everybody's in an uproar and I can't hang around long enough to see it all sorted out. I've got to go—I'm late for a meeting now. We'll figure everything out later."

Those beautiful green eyes widened trustingly. "We will?"

Damn, she was beautiful. He forced a matter-of-fact tone. "Sure, if you want to."

"I want to," she said.

"Now see here," Linnell blustered, "I'm not used to having people walk out on me. You stay right where you are until—"

"Sorry," Zane said, but he wasn't. He did have an appointment; he *was* late. But even more, he needed to get away from here before he did something drastic, like punching the man in the nose.

Or said something that would get him into even more trouble than he was in already, which was considerable.

CHAPTER FOUR

DARA watched her grandfather devour his eggs Benedict while she picked at a fruit salad and dry toast. Around them rose the dignified hum of polite conversation and the rattle of silver and crystal.

Not for Donald Linnell a trip through one of Las Vegas's many buffets. He'd insisted on a real restaurant complete with linen tablecloths and bowing waiters. It didn't matter to Dara where they went; she knew she wouldn't be able to eat a bite.

Her stomach was in revolt and her nerves were in overdrive. This time, she'd done it, she'd really done it. She'd challenged her grandfather in a way guaranteed to create repercussions.

She wished Zane were here. Sighing, she prodded a chunk of fresh peach around the plate with her fork. Was he telling the truth when he insisted he didn't remember a thing about their adventures the night before? Surely not, and yet...

He had seemed sincerely confused this morning. Maybe he'd already been drunk when she entered the Golden Gringo. That thought hadn't occurred to her at the time. He hadn't seemed to be drinking much—a few beers—but different people reacted differently to alcohol, didn't they? Perhaps she should speak to Slim about that. He might know how—

''So,'' her grandfather announced, placing his knife

and fork on his empty plate and managing to yank her from her jumbled thoughts, "what have you to say for yourself, young lady?"

Dara kept her voice calm and level. "Nothing, Grandfather. I'm married now and you might as well accept it."

His eyes narrowed. "You think so, do you?"

Giving up all pretense of eating, she placed her own fork on the table. "That's how it is. I finally found the one man you can't buy off or frighten away and I married him."

"And you've known this paragon of virtue…how long? Twenty-four hours?"

She felt her cheeks burn; she'd known Zane considerably less, actually. "Long enough," she said, raising her chin defiantly.

"Princess, Princess." He used her childhood nickname while shaking his head unhappily. Just then, the waiter appeared to remove the dishes, and Donald waited until they were alone before continuing. "Don't you know I'm just trying to look out for your best interests?"

"In your own way, I suppose, but—"

"And that I love you?"

She caught her breath. "I love you, too, Grandfather, but I can't live my life forever under your thumb."

Donald signaled for more coffee. "I would think that with your father's sorry example added to your sister's disastrous experiment in independence, you'd be grateful for my guidance."

"It's not guidance, it's interference. Besides, I'm

not *them.* Father had been married and divorced twice by the time he was my age and twice more before he died. You can hardly compare me to him. As for Blythe—she was twenty years old when she eloped. I'm twenty-five, which is an adult by any standard.''

''You think you're acting like an adult when you marry a stranger?'' His face contorted. ''I should have been more vigilant.''

''Zane's the best thing that ever happened to me,'' she said, suddenly struck by the realization that this statement of hope could turn out to be true.

''You couldn't be more wrong for each other, Princess.'' Reaching across the small table, he patted her hand and gave her his most winsome smile. ''As much as I love you, I'm not unaware of your short-comings. You're spoiled and headstrong and impul-sive.''

''Thank you for sharing that,'' she retorted, stung by his assessment—and just a little afraid that at least part of it might be true. She'd heard the same criti-cisms of her character all her life and they'd taken a toll.

''I'm sorry,'' he said, ''but it's true. I don't deny that I may be partly to blame, but I remain determined to—to save you, from yourself if necessary.''

''Even if I don't want to be saved?'' she cried.

''Especially then. Nor can we continue to ignore the fact that you're in line for a considerable inheri-tance. Believe me, the men I've protected you from have been well aware of that.''

''Zane isn't,'' she said proudly. ''That's certainly not why he married me.''

"Then why *did* he?" Donald asked bluntly.

"Why, b-because…" She didn't have a clue why he'd married her unless, as she was beginning to suspect, he'd been drunk and didn't know *what* he was doing. And what would that say about his character, not to mention her chances of making their marriage work?

"At least we both know why *you* married him," Donald said. "You were on the rebound—and you wanted to hurt me."

"Hurt you! That's not it at all." And it wasn't. Escape him, yes. Hurt him? Never deliberately. She hadn't even thought it in her power to do so, since he had always seemed so all-powerful and self-sufficient.

He raised thick, white-frosted brows in a cynical gesture. "Then what? Do you really expect me to believe this is a case of love at first sight? Are you your father's daughter after all?"

Love? The possible truth shocked her. "I didn't say that," she denied, adding lamely, "It…it just seemed right at the time. Maybe it *was* fate."

Donald made a face, then dropped his napkin on the table. "It could also be temporary insanity. You won't be thinking about fate if you wake up one fine morning with no husband, no money and no self-respect. I'm trying to spare you that."

She rose. "I don't need or want your help."

He also stood up. "You'll always need my help. What experience do you have, living in the real world? You're a hothouse flower, my darling granddaughter. You don't know what it's like out here in the trenches."

"I can take care of myself," she said staunchly, but she felt a shiver of doubt. Could she? Really? She added quickly, "And I'll have Zane to help me."

Donald's smile was chilly. "Will you? Where is your new husband at this moment? Apparently not thinking about you or—"

The interruption of a waiter offered a welcome respite. "Mrs. Farley?"

"I'm afraid you have the wrong..." Dara gasped. "That's me!" She laughed incredulously.

"I have a message for you." The waiter extended an envelope.

She opened the flap and extracted a single sheet of hotel stationery. Her heart stopped beating. Was Zane writing to tell her goodbye? She realized she was a lot of trouble to him, but he'd known all about her family situation when he'd offered to marry her—that is, if he remembered any of what she'd told him. Had her grandfather won yet again?

Heart in her throat, she unfolded the paper and read the note, first quickly to herself and then out loud.

"Sorry I had to scoot out on you like that this morning. I'll leave two tickets in your name at the box office for this afternoon's rodeo. We'll talk later.

                                        Zane"

"See?" she cried triumphantly. "He *is* thinking of me!"

"But not with love," Donald said softly. "That

could be a note written by the milkman. Face it, Dara. This is a farce and we all know it.''

Maybe to him it was a farce, she stewed while she led the way out of the restaurant. To her it was much, much more serious. Perhaps because of her grandfather's opposition or perhaps because of the man she'd married so impulsively, she wasn't ready to give up or give in.

She was a married woman. She intended to stay that way.

When Dara and Donald arrived at the box office of the Thomas and Mack Center on the campus of the University of Nevada, Las Vegas, she was delighted to find Slim loitering nearby, obviously waiting for her. Throwing her arms around him, she hugged him in gratitude.

He grinned at her a bit cautiously. ''That's quite a welcome, Dary.''

''Dary?'' her grandfather echoed incredulously.

Dara laughed. ''That's what he calls me, Grandfather. This is Zane's friend, Slim. Slim, this is my—''

''Howdy, howdy!'' Slim grabbed Donald's hand and pumped it enthusiastically. ''Mighty glad to meet the grandpa of this fine little gal.''

Donald retrieved his hand and looked Slim over with caution. The two men, although approximately the same height and build, could not have looked more different. Where Donald wore expensive, coordinated sportswear, Slim was arrayed in what Dara now recognized as the cowboy uniform: jeans, a long-sleeved plaid shirt, beat-up black hat and boots with run-over heels.

It was an obvious case of the sophisticate and the country cornball, and Dara was more than grateful for the cornball's unswerving support.

"What are you doing here?" she gushed. "How did you know we were coming? Did Zane send you? Are you going to the rodeo with us?"

"Figured I better." Slim answered the last question first, tucking her hand beneath the crook of his arm. "I got a notion you don't know diddly about rodeo, am I right?"

"Welll…" She gave him a friendly grin. "Maybe a little less than diddly."

Slim turned his brightly inquisitive glance on her grandfather. "How about you, Don? You ever been to one a these clambakes?"

"I haven't had that privilege," Donald admitted very tongue in cheek.

Slim nodded. "I figured. Wal, follow me, folks, and I'll tell you all about it."

With Dara on his arm, he threaded his way through the crowd, leaving Donald to follow in their wake.

The crowd overwhelmed Dara with both its size and enthusiasm. "This is a world I never even knew existed," she confessed to Slim.

"Rodeo's big and gettin' bigger," he said with satisfaction. "This'un is the biggest of 'em all—the National Finals. These are only the top cowboys in each event and they're goin' for big prize money— more than three million this year. Them old boys blow

in here loaded for bear and that brings the fans with
'em.''

Even Donald looked impressed. "Three million
dollars, huh."

Dara watched the cowboys milling around at one
end of the dirt-floored arena. A few others were already mounted on their horses; they seemed to be riding around inspecting the surface upon which they'd
be competing. "What are the events?" she asked.
And before she could censor her words, she added,
"What are Zane's events?" Nuts. She shouldn't have
asked that question. Now her grandfather would realize how little she knew about her new husband.

As if he didn't already.

"Zane's a roper and a bulldogger," Slim said.
"Sometimes he also team ropes, but he didn't qualify
in that this year. The other events are saddle bronc
riding, bull riding—"

"Thank God he doesn't do *that!*" Dara exclaimed,
appalled at the thought.

Slim laughed. "He don't now, but he messed
around with it when he was a sprout. Lotta ranch boys
do. Anyway, to go on, we also got bareback riding
and—what'd I leave out?" He counted on his fingers.
"Barrel racing. That's for the gals."

Dara frowned. "Tell me about the…you called it
steer wrestling? Why on earth would a man wrestle a
steer?"

Slim gave her a whimsical grin. "Why is there
air?" he asked rhetorically. His eyes twinkled. "The
idee is to grab the critter's horns and flip him over
onto his side. It can get real excitin', lemme tell you."

That didn't sound like a good idea to Dara, but before she could respond, music blared. The crowd roared, welcoming what Slim called the "grand entry" of riders around the arena. And then she saw Zane, her gaze drawn to him as if he was riding in a spotlight. How straight he sat in the saddle of his horse, a sleek red animal prancing along with its neck arched.

She felt like a teenage girl staring at some rock star, not a woman looking at her husband.

Only he really wasn't…not yet anyway. If she had her way, though, he would be—and soon.

Zane caught, threw and tied his calf in 6.4 seconds.

"That's good, isn't it?" Dara demanded of Slim. Her hands were red from applauding and her throat hoarse from cheering.

Zane had earned those cheers. He rode like a centaur, leaped from his saddle with the agility of a gymnast, picked up the calf on the end of his rope as if it weighed no more than a pound of hamburger and tossed it down, whereupon he proceeded to tie three of its legs so quickly his hands were a blur. Remounting the red horse, he lifted his hat in a graceful salute to the roaring crowd.

"Yep," Slim agreed, "that's good all right. Puts him into first place, but we'll have to wait and see if it holds up."

It did. Zane won the calf roping, much to Dara's excitement. Turning to her grandfather, she hugged him. "He won!" she cried. "Isn't he wonderful?"

"Wonderful," Donald agreed dryly. "Unfortunately, there's not too much call for calf chasing."

"You mean in *your* circles," she retorted. "I've got a new circle where it's highly valued."

"You're really getting into this rodeo thing," he replied, a puzzled expression on his face. "Just be careful, Princess. You don't belong in that world and you never will. I don't want to see you get hurt."

"I'm a big girl and I'm willing to take the chance." At that moment, she felt very much in control. She could do this. She could watch her husband rope calves as if she'd been doing it all her life.

Then the first steer wrestler was called and Dara stared in disbelief. Zane was going to do that? She wasn't sure she could stand it! When Slim had explained the whole thing, she hadn't imagined that the steer would be so big or run so fast, or that not one but two cowboys on horseback would chase the huge animal at breakneck speed.

As she watched wide-eyed, one of the riders threw himself into the air and caught those curving horns, thrust his stiff legs forward and dug his heels into the dirt of the arena floor. The steer, naturally, had no interest in stopping, and the heels of the cowboy's boots dug long furrows as he tried to put on the brakes. Then the cowboy wrestled that enormous animal onto its side on the ground. It didn't seem humanly possible, yet many of them managed to do it—most in less than ten seconds.

The announcer called Zane's name.

Dara started from her seat. She wasn't sure she wanted to watch this.

Her grandfather rose with her. "Here," he said, sliding an arm around her waist, "we don't have to stay if you don't want to."

Slim grabbed her hand and tugged. "No self-respectin' wife would run out on her husband thataway," he said, his steady gaze boring into her face. "This is what Zane *does* and if you cain't stand to see it, you don't belong with him, fate be hanged."

Dara darted a confused glance from the old cowboy to her grandfather. "But—"

"But me no buts," Slim shot back. "In case you ain't heard, it's as easy to get divorced in this town as it is to get married. Still, you do what you gotta do, Dary."

Releasing her hand, he turned back toward the arena, pointedly ignoring her. For a moment, she hesitated, feeling the pull of her grandfather's grip on her arm. Then without another word, she sank back onto her seat beside Slim. He was right and she knew it. She would watch. She had to.

The steer sprang forward. When it reached the designated head start, the barrier holding back the two mounted men tripped and their horses leaped out of the chutes at a dead run. In a couple of jumps, Zane's red horse reached the steer's side. Without hesitation, he launched himself toward the big head of the animal, his hands reaching for the curved horns.

Reaching, grazing—falling under the animal's neck headfirst and right into the path of the running horse ridden by the man Slim had identified as something called the hazer, there to make sure the steer ran straight. The horse bucked and jumped, nearly unseating his own rider. The crowd let out a collective gasp, then an ''Ahhh'' when it looked as if the pounding hooves had missed the rolling man.

Zane came to his feet, his hat still firmly on his head and his left arm held bent tightly at his waist. Lifting his hat in a salute to the crowd, he turned to trot back toward the chutes.

Donald leaned close to his daughter. ''Dara, are you all right? You're white as a sheet.''

She lifted her chin and sucked in a calming breath. ''I'm fine,'' she said with admirable firmness. ''Slim, what does it mean when they miss the cow entirely?''

The old cowboy laughed. ''Generally, it means they ain't payin' attention,'' he said, chortling. ''Now what do you suppose could be on that cowboy's mind?''

Working with only one hand, Zane yanked the saddle off his horse and tossed it over a bale of hay against the wall, all the while swearing under his breath. The sorrel gelding, Scout, looked around with as close to a frown as a horse was likely to get.

''Sorry, fella,'' Zane apologized, adding a firm pat on the animal's neck. ''I just made a fool out of myself, but you're in the clear. I think everybody could see it wasn't *your* fault.''

Shorty, Zane's hazer, grunted agreement. ''That's for danged sure. I don't know where your mind was, but it sure wasn't on that—waaait a minute!'' Shorty paused to lean against the side of his big black horse. ''I almost forgot you're a married man now. Thinkin' about the little woman instead of business?''

''What do *you* think?'' It came out a snarl.

"I think…" Shorty considered. "I think if some-body had told me Zane Farley would marry a woman the same night he met her, I'da sold everything I owned and put the money agin it! Hell, I'd even a sold my horse." He plucked off the saddle, adding to the horse, "No offense, Wall-Eye."

"Yeah, well, I'd have taken some of that bet my-self," Zane said bleakly. Protecting his arm, he led his horse to a stall, opened the door and turned him in.

"Looks like that tumble didn't do that left arm a yours a whole lot of good," Shorty observed, releas-ing his own horse into a stall.

"Now there's a news flash." Zane rubbed his throbbing elbow.

Shorty fished around in the pocket of his jeans. "I got some pain pills here—"

"You!" Zane turned on his friend. "You're the one who gave me those pain pills last night." He grabbed the small packet and glared at it.

"Well, yeah, sure. You was hurtin'." Shorty frowned. "It helped, in case you don't remember."

"That's just it. I *don't* remember. What the hell are these things?" Zane peered at the unmarked envelope.

Shorty shrugged. "I dunno exactly. My sister's husband's dentist give 'em to him when he had six teeth pulled."

Zane groaned. He must have been crazy to take one of these mystery pills last night. Thanks to Shorty's sister's husband's dentist and a couple of beers, Zane's life would never be the same.

"So how is the little woman?" Shorty asked slyly.

"She's here." Zane knew she'd used the tickets because he'd checked, although he'd made sure she didn't see him. "Uh…about last night, Shorty…"

"What about it?" The cowboy hung his horse's bridle over the saddle horn.

"I'm a little fuzzy on the details," Zane said carefully. "I've been trying to remember…you know, which one of us…me or Dara, I mean…which one of us brought up *marriage* first."

"It was you," Shorty said clearly and calmly. "As I recall, you said something about savin' her from her big bad granddaddy or some such. She thought you was cute—I could tell that easy enough, but she wasn't buyin'. Then Slim give her that quarter and she hit the jackpot and everybody agreed it was fate and—why you lookin' so green around the gills, Zane? You need to see a doctor or what?"

Zane just shook Shorty off and headed down the corridor toward the exit. Of all the things he hadn't wanted to hear, that was at the top of his list: that he, not Dara, was to blame for this fiasco. If he'd gotten her into this, it was damn well up to him to get her out.

The only question was…*how?*

He walked outside still deep in thought. He didn't want to hurt her and he didn't want anyone else to hurt her, either. There was something so vulnerable about her, so trusting…

And as if he'd conjured her up, she was in his arms before he knew what had hit him—Dara, his wife, a woman he barely knew. Shocked, he held her close and stared into her smiling face. Her green eyes sparkled and those luscious lips curved in a smile.

"You were wonderful," she whispered, her fingers digging into his shoulder. "I was so proud of you!"

Rising on tiptoe, she pressed her soft lips against his in a quick, shy kiss that set off a million alarm bells inside him. Before he could get his wits about him enough to grab her, she'd slipped from his embrace.

"Dinner tonight in our suite?" she asked, her expression both hopeful and guarded. "I hope you don't mind—we have to make grandfather understand."

Without waiting for an answer, she whirled away.

Stunned, he watched her hurry to join her grandfather and Slim, waiting for her near the gate. Linnell was glaring; Slim was beaming.

Reaching them, Dara turned to send him a final wave. It was a sunny day and she stood as if in a spotlight, her blond hair lighting sparks.

He rubbed one hand across his mouth where her lips had so briefly touched. He thought he could still feel the imprint of her, which was ridiculous. He should be thinking of a way to let her down easy, dammit. Instead, he was thinking about—

With a sharp expletive, he turned in the opposite direction to the one she'd taken.

CHAPTER FIVE

A TENSE trio came together late that night in Dara's hotel suite. Zane thought Dara looked as uncomfortable as he felt, while her grandfather looked grimly determined.

Was she, too, remembering that impulsive little kiss? It seemed unlikely and yet…

"I took the liberty of ordering dinner," Donald Linnell announced. "It should arrive any minute. I hope no one minds."

Zane didn't think Dara's grandfather looked as if he gave a hoot in hell whether anybody minded or not. Nevertheless, he shrugged. "Suits me. I'm not here to eat anyway."

Dara gave him an uncertain smile. "I'm not even sure I *can* eat. Uh…Zane, thank you for the rodeo tickets. I've never been to a rodeo before. I found it very exciting."

He couldn't stop the corners of his mouth twitching in an answering smile. "Did you understand what was going on?"

"Oh, yes." Her smile was both charming and disarming. "Slim was with us and he explained everything."

She looked so eager to please that Zane felt himself softening toward her. "Everything, huh." The smile tugging at his mouth broke loose.

She nodded, then bit her lower lip. "I was so proud when you won the calf roping but...I...uh...hope you weren't hurt when you...uh—you know."

"Missed my steer?" he supplied, amused at her reluctance to say it. He'd been embarrassed when it happened, then mad as hell at himself, but her diffidence now was almost endearing. Under no circumstances would he mention his throbbing elbow as an excuse.

"Did that horse step on you?" Her worry crept through in the wrinkled brow.

"Yep, but don't give it too much worry. It's not exactly the first time."

A knock on the door signaled the arrival of the waiter with a cart swathed in white linen. While Dara saw to the arrangement of the meal, Zane walked to the window and looked out over the glittering nightlife of Las Vegas.

They were all being so civilized, he thought with disgust. Dara and her grandfather appeared to be on the best of terms. She was probably softening him up. Soon she would announce that their "marriage" had been a mistake, that she and her grandfather had settled their differences and all she wanted from her stand-in husband was a divorce as quickly achieved as that farce of a wedding had been.

When she asked, he'd graciously agree and this whole thing—was it a nightmare or something else?—would be over. Beneath that appealing exterior and vulnerable manner, she was just another poor little rich girl intent upon wrapping her granddaddy around her pinkie. Zane had been handy, nothing more.

This he didn't need. Just as long as nobody insulted him, they could have anything they wanted, he decided, turning away from the window. The sooner this was over with, the better.

But he didn't think it had been very nice of her to kiss him like that.

Zane put down his knife and fork and pushed his plate away. "Good chow," he said, following his words with a prodigious yawn. "I'm beat. Got another big day tomorrow, so if nobody's got anything to say, I think I'll hit the hay."

Dara held her breath, darting a glance at her grandfather. Would he let the whole thing drop? All through the meal, she'd waited for him to launch an attack and he hadn't. Could it be this easy?

It couldn't. Donald Linnell leaned forward, his expression suddenly growing tight and determined. "Just a minute, Farley. We have a few little matters to clear up first."

Zane's gaze remained level and calm. "Such as?"

"Such as—what do you mean to do about my granddaughter?"

A small smile touched the corner of Zane's well-shaped mouth. "What do I mean to do?" He cocked his head. "I'd say that's up to her."

Both men turned to Dara. Resisting an impulse to flinch before two such level gazes, she lifted her chin. "Grandfather, I don't think my marriage need concern you. Zane and I—"

"There is no Zane and you," Donald interrupted impatiently. "You did this to get back at me and we all know it. You've made your point. Don't compound your error by pretending this has the slightest chance to be a real marriage."

Aware of the panicky thrumming of her heart, Dara still had the presence of mind to declare, "It *could* be real. I want it to be real." She looked directly into her grandfather's eyes. "I swear to you, I didn't get married on a lark or to spite you, no matter how it may seem."

At a soft, incredulous exclamation from Zane, she swung her attention in his direction. Was that shock on his face? Before she could decide, he turned his head away and she could no longer see his expression at all. But surely he realized she wasn't going to fall in with her grandfather's wishes?

"Princess," Donald said in a condescending tone, "be reasonable. I'm sure Farley here is willing—hell, he's *eager* to get out of this mess. I've already checked and an annulment or a divorce will be a piece of cake. Then I'll take you back home where you belong and we can work everything out."

"You know we can't!" She twisted her hands together in her lap. "Your idea of compromise is for me to do exactly what you say, but I'm through with that. I'm not your little princess anymore. I'm all grown-up, but just as important, I'm a married woman."

"Yes, yes." He brushed her protests away as if they were of no consequence. "We'll get around to all that, but in the meantime…" He reached into his hip pocket and withdrew a leather checkbook, then opened it with a flourish. "Name your price, Farley—within reason, of course." He waited, pen poised.

Zane didn't react at first. Dara waited for him to laugh, to refuse, to do *something,* but he just sat there with his shoulder toward them and his head turned away. Could it be that he was no different from Blake and all the others her grandfather had bought off or scared away? Her nerves stretched to screaming tautness, she felt her heart constrict more with every passing second.

At last Zane turned, very slowly and deliberately. As his face came into view, Dara gasped and recoiled in her chair. She had never seen such outrage, so hot and angry that it almost singed her where she sat.

Donald also shrank back but caught himself and faced the furious cowboy with stiff shoulders. Their gazes met and clashed. The older man looked away first.

"I meant no disrespect," Donald said finally. "You deserve something for your time."

"I deserve *a lot* for my time," Zane corrected, "but I've put in damned little at this point."

"All the more reason to cut your losses," Donald said quickly, flourishing his pen. "You—"

"That's it." Zane stood up abruptly, the chilly light still shining from his dark eyes but his voice level. "It's been a helluva day and I'm worn out. Dara, why don't you see your grandfather out and then come on to bed. Linnell, we'll talk again tomorrow if you want to, but I wouldn't advise you to insult me again."

Zane walked into the bedroom and closed the door. Dara watched his long-legged stride with awe, thinking that she'd never seen anybody with the nerve to turn his back on her grandfather before.

"Grandfather," she said, "you'd better do as he says."

"Forget what he says. Come with me, Princess. You don't want to stay here with *him*."

"Oh, yes, I do!" And it was true. *Come on to bed,* he'd said. Did that mean he was ready to make this a real marriage?

"Don't push me too far."

He was angry now. She sighed. "I'm sorry to disappoint you, but I'm staying."

"That does disappoint me." Donald rose abruptly. "This isn't over yet," he added. "I'm a man used to having his own way."

"I know that, Grandfather." She went to walk with him to the door although she longed to run instead to her husband's safe arms. "You're an irresistible force, but this time, you've met an immovable object."

At least, she thought, closing the door behind him, *I hope so.*

Stepping inside the bedroom, Dara quickly closed the door behind her and leaned against it. Her glance darted around the room and she held her breath.

And realized finally that he wasn't there. What had she expected, that he'd be waiting for her in bed? How silly she was being!

Then he walked out of the bathroom and she couldn't breathe. He'd taken off his shirt but still wore his jeans and that wide, tooled leather belt with the huge silver buckle, his boots and his spurs. She stared at his tapered waist and broad chest, brown and smooth and firmly muscled, as were his arms.

After admiring the parts, she admired the whole: long legs swathed in faded denim, narrow hips and a flat, muscled abdomen. Tall, powerful as a stalking lion, he crossed the room to sit on the edge of the bed.

She stood there with her heart in her throat, wondering what she should do next—knowing that what she wanted to do was throw herself into his arms and thank him for standing up to her grandfather, for wanting her, for...

He looked up suddenly, and instead of desire, she thought she saw irritation on his lean face. "What the hell was that all about?" He jerked his head toward the other room almost accusingly.

"My grandfather?" She didn't know what she should do, so she took a seat in a padded chair facing him. "That's how he is. I told you, remember? He thinks he can buy or bluff his way to everything he—"

"Not him," Zane interrupted. "You. *Him* I understood."

"Me?" She stared at him, mystified.

"I gave you a ready-made out and you didn't grab it. I'm wondering why."

"Out of what?"

"Out of this so-called marriage." He shoved his hands through already disheveled hair, fingers splayed. He looked tired and perhaps a little perplexed. "You've got the upper hand with your grandfather now, so what are you waiting for? I was prepared to be a gentleman and let you save face by leaving the choice up to you. You blindsided me."

"I didn't!"

"You sure as hell did. 'It *could* be real. I want it to be real.'" He repeated the words she'd said earlier to her grandfather, adding, "Just exactly how am I supposed to take that?"

"Figure it out for yourself!" Stung, she glared at him.

He shook his head decisively. "Not me. That's what gets me in trouble in the first place, thinking I can figure out a woman."

Dara chewed on her lower lip. She'd been honest with him about her reasons for being willing to marry a perfect stranger: the willingness to risk everything to get out from beneath her grandfather's thumb. If Zane had been equally honest with her, he'd gone along out of some sense of chivalry.

In fact, thinking back, Slim and the others who knew him best had seemed astonished that he'd taken the plunge. Apparently, he had a reputation as a lone wolf, so far as permanent commitments to women went.

So here she was, infatuated and moving quickly toward something more. If she threw that in his face, he'd probably jump up off that bed and run as far and as fast as those long, lean legs would carry him.

But if she played on his chivalrous nature...

She choked back a calculated sob.

He looked appalled. "There's nothing to cry about," he protested.

"Oh, no?" She swallowed tears that threatened to become all too real. "You want out."

"Don't *you?* You've got your grandfather eating out of your hand, so why go on with this charade?"

Because I don't think it would be a charade, given half a chance! "Because," she said in a quivering voice, "nothing's changed. My grandfather will get his own way again. Every time he does, it's that much harder for me the next time."

"Oh, for…!" Zane pulled off his boots and flexed long, narrow feet in gray socks. "Just what is it your grandfather does that gives him all this power and money?"

"He has his own import/export company in San Francisco."

"I see. And what do *you* do when you're not eloping?"

She hung her head. "I work for him at Global headquarters. That's his company—Global Import/Export."

"And you live…?"

She sighed. "With him and my sister, Blythe, and her little girl."

He arched dark brows. "No brother-in-law?"

"No." She chewed on her lower lip. "Blythe eloped at twenty and was back home at twenty-one with a baby, which meant she'd forfeited her inheritance. Her husband had swindled her out of every other penny she had. She was destitute and grateful to Grandfather for taking care of her and Jenny, but the experience…well, it broke her spirit, Zane. I feel so sorry for her.''

He looked thoughtful. ''I suppose your grandfather considers her a horrible example of what could happen to his other granddaughter, while you see a horrible example of what giving in to him does.''

He did understand. She gave him a relieved smile. ''I love my grandfather, Zane, but he's ruining my life. If I were a stronger person, I wouldn't need you or anyone to…well, run interference for me. Besides, I…'' She hesitated, watching the defensive gleam spark in his dark eyes.

How many women had put moves on this man? she wondered suddenly. He was as handsome as a movie star and that was just for starters. He was also chivalrous and strong and she could easily join what must surely be a throng of female admirers.

But not if she wanted her chance with him. She forced a bright smile. ''I like you and Slim and Shorty and the rest of your friends. I know I'm a fish out of water in your world, but I'd like a chance to see if I can learn how to fit in. I promise you I'll be the best wife I possibly can if you're willing to stand by me now.''

For a long moment, he simply looked at her, his eyes stormy and troubled. Then he said, ''I've got to think about this.''

He crossed the room and opened the sliding mirrored closet door. Stretching, he dragged a fluffy blue blanket from the top shelf. With it tucked under his arm, he headed for the door.

''Zane!'' She stood up. ''Where are you going?''

"To sleep on the sofa."

"But…" She looked at the bed and then back at him. "You told me to meet you in bed, or something to that effect. Why…?"

He laughed, but it had a grim ring to it. "That was for your grandfather's benefit. See you in the morning, Dara. We'll talk then."

Talk? Talk! She didn't want to talk anymore, not about their future or anything else. The time for talk was past. She'd married him in good faith. The likelihood that he might walk out on her was even more wounding than Blake's defection had been.

But maybe he wouldn't. Maybe he'd stand by her until she had a chance to win him over. Maybe it *was* fate at work after all….

She could only hope.

"All right," Zane said across the breakfast table set up in their suite, "here's what we're going to do. I'll—" A pounding on the door made him clench his teeth in what looked very much like frustration. He glared at her. "Son of a…! Doesn't your grandfather ever get tired of barging in uninvited?"

"No," she said honestly.

"Then you might as well go let him in."

"He'll get in under his own power."

A couple of seconds later, Donald Linnell marched into the sitting room, his expression faintly triumphant. He carried an expensive leather briefcase, which he placed on the floor near the table before pulling out a chair and sitting down uninvited.

"Good morning," he said. "I'll have some coffee, Dara."

She poured. "Grandfather, you've interrupted us. Perhaps we could meet you later at the—"

"I'm here. I'll stay." He took the cup and saucer from her numb fingers. He was all business this morning, as if he'd figured everything out to his satisfaction. "So what have you two decided?"

"We were just about to discuss that," Dara admitted, darting an anxious little glance toward her taciturn bridegroom.

"In that case," Donald said, "I'm in time." Reaching for his briefcase, he unbuckled the flap and extracted several folders, which he placed before him on the breakfast table.

Zane buttered a biscuit, then slathered on strawberry jam. He indicted the files with a dip of his head. "I'm almost afraid to ask."

"No need to ask. I'll tell you." Donald lifted the top file and waved it around. "This is a report from a detective agency I hired to find out about the Farleys of Colorado."

Zane started and a look of hot resentment touched his face. "Why, you arrogant son of a…" He stopped himself with a smile completely lacking in humor.

He followed that with a quick, sympathetic glance at Dara that said clearly, to her at least, *I'm beginning to see what you're up against.*

"Not to fear," Donald went on airily. "Your family checks out as decent, hardworking ranchers." He laughed. "No insanity or criminal activity that my man could come up with, at least not in twenty-four hours.''

''Well, hell,'' Zane said in a disgusted tone, ''I'm relieved he didn't dig up Grandpa John.''

Donald shot the other man a sharp glance. ''Dig him up? Where's he gone? Has he got something he'd prefer to hide?''

''Just about everything,'' Zane drawled. ''He's been dead for twenty-four years.''

Dara gave a brief sputter of nervous laughter. She didn't know if her grandfather had fallen for it, but she sure had.

''Yes, well…'' Donald cleared his throat, his expression indignant. ''The Farleys check out, but that still doesn't prove you're not after my granddaughter's inheritance.''

''Grandfather!'' Her cheeks burned with shame. ''Can't you imagine a man would want me for reasons other than money? Besides which—I haven't got any, or at least not much, and you know it very well. My trust fund is tied up in more red tape than I'll ever get through.''

Donald smiled. ''Which brings us to the next topic.'' He put down the first file and picked up the second. ''What I have here is a complete revision of the conditions surrounding your trust fund.''

She groaned. ''How could you possibly make it any more difficult for me to get to that money than it already is?''

''More difficult? No.'' He shook his head for emphasis. ''I'm making it easier. If you come home with me now, I'm prepared to begin releasing the interest on your trust fund now, instead of making you wait until you're thirty.''

"Thirty!'' Zane looked flabbergasted. "You'd do that to your own granddaughter?''

"I see you don't know the details of Dara's financial situation,'' Donald said smoothly. "Does that make a difference to you? Because if it does, I've got more bad news.''

"I think I can take it,'' Zane said dryly, popping half a biscuit into his mouth. He seemed to have got past his initial reaction and now merely looked bemused.

Dara, on the other hand, was shaken. There was a lot she could do with that money. She could rent or buy a place of her own, not necessarily even in San Francisco. She could quit her job with Global and find work she could enjoy; she could travel as she'd always longed to do; she could even help her sister and niece.

If she didn't have a husband, of course.

Not that it really mattered, because there had to be a catch. She met her grandfather's veiled gaze, her own steady. "Go on,'' she said, her mouth dry.

"Either you end this farce and come home to me, at which point I'll begin a gradual release of your money, or—''

"Or what?''

"Or at the earliest possible moment—which will be the day you walk out on this alleged marriage— I'll liquidate the entire amount and cut you off without a dime. That's it.''

"Just like you did with Blythe,'' Dara said faintly.

Their father had left that money to them, even if he'd left it encumbered by a multitude of conditions. Even so, Dara had never expected to be totally deprived of it.

She supposed Blythe had been equally shocked.

"Just like Blythe," he agreed. "It's for your own good after all."

"But—but…" She stumbled for a response. "It's too late even if I wanted to take you up on your offer. There's that stipulation about divorce. Now that I'm legally married—"

"I haven't suggested divorce," he said smugly. "Annulment. There's a world of difference."

Zane leaned forward, frowning. *"What the hell are you two talking about?"*

His annoyed question sent Dara's heart off on another rocket. She had no idea how he'd take the details, so she chose the coward's way out. "You explain, Grandfather."

"Glad to." He gave Zane a sly glance. "According to the trust funds set up by my son for his daughters, they receive a hefty sum on their thirtieth birthdays *if* they have never been divorced. If they have, the entire amount is forfeited to be used at my discretion. I also have control of all income generated by the principal."

Zane looked disgusted. "That's—that's inhuman. What father would do such a thing to his own flesh and blood?"

"A father who wanted his children to overcome his own weaknesses and escape his own mistakes,"

Donald said. "My son was a fool for the opposite sex, an absolute fool. That predilection ruined his life."

In a disgusted tone, Zane said, "Well, hell!" He pinned Dara with his unruly gaze. "None of this makes a lick of sense to me, but it's up to you. If you want to make the best deal you can with him, I won't get in your way."

She shook her head violently. "I don't care if he *gives* the money away. It's been held in front of me like a carrot on a stick ever since my father's death and that was eleven years ago."

"You mean you really want to take a crack at this marriage stuff? Think carefully, Dara."

Their gazes met, but she couldn't read his feelings in his eyes. Gathering up all her courage, she nodded wordlessly.

He drew a deep breath. "That's it, then."

Her heart leaped. "You mean it? Really?"

"Really. But if it doesn't work out—" his gaze bored into her as if he needed to be sure she understood "—you'll pay a helluva price."

Donald interrupted by banging a fist on the table. "If you knew how much money we're talking about here, you wouldn't be so eager to write it off," he threw at Zane.

Who didn't blink an eye. "Don't know, don't care."

"She'll never fit into your world," Donald pressed the argument. "She's a city girl. She's never even been around animals, she's never lived in the country, she's—she's *expensive.*"

"Stuff a sock in it, Linnell." Zane leaned forward

and caught Dara's cold hands in his. "Say it again so everybody knows you mean it."

She licked her lips and spoke firmly. "I mean it."

"Maybe you want to think about it for a few minutes. If you go back, sounds to me like you'll get just about everything you want. If you stick with me, it's a gamble at best. Your grandpa's right when he says you'll be walking into a completely different life."

She felt herself drifting into the fathomless depths of his dark eyes. "I know all that," she said, surprised by her own calm. "We're married. I want to stay married…for the rest of my life."

"Dara!" Donald's voice was sharp. "If you cling to this cockamamy marriage, you're on your own. You'll get nothing from me, nothing. No allowance—"

"No wife of mine would accept an allowance," Zane cut in, voice sharp as an ice shard.

"Good, because there'll be none of that. Princess—" Donald's tone turned pleading "—you'll have to depend on your husband for everything. You don't want that."

"Don't I?" Her full attention remained focused on Zane as she looked for the slightest indication that he was just baiting her grandfather. She saw none. This was all terrifying to her—the thought of putting her entire future into the hands of a stranger. Still, everything in her shouted that it was the right thing to do…if she had the courage to see it through.

Did she?

She took a deep breath. Both men leaned forward, waiting for her answer.

CHAPTER SIX

"WHEN Zane and I married," Dara said slowly, "it wasn't a joke to me even though we'd just met. I meant every word I said, including the part about 'till death us do part'."

She didn't know who looked more shocked by that revelation, her grandfather or her bridegroom. Trying to head off reproach, she rushed on. "I know I'm romantic and sentimental and maybe even a total ditz, Grandfather, like you've told me all my life. But I felt as if maybe fate really was at work, just the way Slim said."

"Darling, Princess..." Donald's face looked gray, as if the possibility of defeat was beginning to sink in. "You don't mean—"

"I do," she said quickly, meeting Zane's gaze. "I know this has been a...well, a whirlwind wedding, but that doesn't mean it can't work."

Zane nodded, his expression grim. "Be very sure this is what you really mean, because once we—"

"Wait a minute, wait a minute!" Donald jumped up. "Dara, I can't believe you're determined to do this crazy thing!"

"I *am* determined, more determined than you can possibly understand." And more than Zane understood, she thought. Given a little time, she had every expectation that the warmth of her feelings toward him would blossom into…something more—she still couldn't use the word *love* even as a potential. Still, she felt in her heart that they had a chance at something truly special.

Donald looked sick. He shook his head groggily, then pulled himself together with considerable effort. He looked at her and the old gleam leaped back into his eyes. "I don't want to lose my little girl," he said grimly, "even knowing it won't be forever."

Dara groaned. "Grandfather, didn't you hear what I said? I'm *talking* about forever."

"I understand that's what you think you mean," he conceded, "but things change. You'll have to come to your senses eventually."

"There's no reasoning with you, apparently."

"Apparently." Donald waved that aside. "When you come to your senses, I want to make it as easy as possible for you to admit it and come back home where you belong."

"You're not listening to me."

"I am. Now you listen to me. I'll give you six months—no, make that a year. If you change your mind within that time, I'll take you back to the bosom of the family, no questions asked. I'll even override the stipulation in your trust fund against divorce."

"What trust fund?" She laughed in disbelief, almost light-headed. She'd never imagined she could feel so little concern for money. "You said I'd never see a dime of it, remember?"

"Yes," he agreed, "and you won't if it comes to that. Tell you what, I'll give you until—" he checked his watch, one of those big gold affairs with dials for everything from temperature to dates to the time in Hong Kong ''—December 15 of next year. That's a year to come to your senses and admit you made a mistake. After that, you'll have to stick strictly to the stipulations your father left, without any help from me.''

Dara felt sorry for him, but every word he said only served to strengthen her resolve. ''Take the money now, Grandfather. I won't be back.''

''Never say never, Dara. A lot can happen in a year.'' Donald stuffed the files back into his briefcase and stood up. ''Remember that I love you. Everything I've done—everything I will do—is for your own good.''

''I love you, too, Grandfather, but everything you've done is for *your* own good, not mine. I have to find my own life.'' Sudden emotion misted her eyes and she blinked tears away.

He took a dragging step toward the door, then swung on Zane. ''Be good to her while you've got her because it won't be for long,'' he ordered fiercely. ''She's on the rebound. If you don't treat her right, you'll answer to me.''

''You can count on it,'' Zane replied in his insolent Western drawl, ''but I have a feeling that I'll be answering to you anyway...sir.''

Dara had that same feeling, but it no longer frightened her. She felt an overpowering sense of relief, actually.

Zane was staring at her, his forehead creased in a frown. She gave him a tentative smile. ''What is it?''

she asked. "You were wonderful. I couldn't have asked for a better champion."

"Thanks," he said gruffly, "but you could ask for a better husband because I don't have the first idea—well, maybe the *first* idea but not a single one after that—about what the hell a husband's supposed to do or be. I never intended to be in a spot where I had to figure it out, either. When the going gets rough—and believe me, it will—remember that this was your doing. I'm just along for the ride."

Walking into the bedroom, he closed the door behind him, leaving his bride to wonder when her world would right itself and stay that way.

Zane slept on the sofa again that night, leaving the bedroom for Dara. Tossing and turning, she asked herself over and over again what she'd do if he told her tomorrow morning that he just didn't want to stay married to her after all, under any circumstances.

She had another worry, as well, one that almost superseded that. And she'd ask him about it—she would, right out, the first chance she got.

A soft tapping on the door awakened her the next morning and she sat up in bed, pushing her tangled hair away from her face. She felt groggy and sleep logged. The tapping continued and she called out a tentative "Come in?"

Zane appeared in the doorway, barefoot and wearing nothing but his Wrangler jeans. The breadth of his chest and the washboard ripples of his midriff were awesome and she couldn't help staring.

"Mornin'," he said gruffly. In return, his gaze

slipped over her, like a warm touch before it moved on. He'd dismissed her. "Just passing through," he added, crossing to the bathroom.

She watched the door close behind him. With a sigh, she stacked the pillows beneath her head and leaned back against them. Frowning and thoughtful, she waited for him to emerge.

She heard the shower running, and a few minutes later, he came out wearing jeans again and toweling wet hair with a sparkling white towel. Without a word, he walked to the battered duffel bag in the corner of the room and pulled out a plaid shirt.

She continued to stare at him while he yanked it over his head without unfastening the buttons. She had to talk to him, but was this the time? On the other hand, what could be gained by waiting? If she had to crawl back to her grandfather, perhaps sooner would be better than—

"What!" He spat the word aggressively, as if it had been forced from him.

Startled, she pulled her gaze from his impressive body to his equally impressive face. "I'm sorry?"

"Why do you keep staring at me as if I were a monkey in the zoo? What's on your mind, lady?"

"I was just wondering…"

"Spit it out." He approached the bed, the shirt hanging unbuttoned around his waist.

She didn't spit it out; she blurted it out. "Are you—*are you gay?*"

His eyes went wide and he stared at her as if she'd asked if he were Martian. "Am I *what?*"

"Gay." Now that it was out, she felt better. "It's

not that I think you *are,* but…we're married
and…and before I get my hopes up about this marriage…'' She'd run out of steam and just looked up
at him with consternation.

"Why," he asked in measured tones, "would you
suggest such a thing?"

She shrugged self-consciously. "Well, we have
been married for two days…and t-two nights. But
you're sleeping in there and I'm sleeping in here
and—"

He moved so fast she had no chance to prepare
before he landed on his belly on the bed beside her,
grabbed her in his arms and rolled over, pulling her
on top of him. "If you're sleeping, you're one up on
me," he muttered, his dark eyes gleaming.

And he kissed her.

With one hand on the back of her head and the
other around her waist, snugging her against the hard
length of him, he kissed her as she had never been
kissed in her life—or ever hoped to be.

When he had finished kissing her, he rolled over,
set her back down on her stack of pillows and rose
from the bed with easy grace. In a state of complete
shock, she stared up at him.

"In answer to your question, I'm not gay." He
grinned, white teeth flashing in his dark face, but she
thought she saw some effort behind it. "What I am
is cautious, or at least I'm trying like hell to be. Your
grandpa was right when he said you're on the rebound. Because of that…because of the way we got
together, we don't know what's going to happen in
the next year. If you decide it's too much effort to

stick it out through the rough times—and there'll be
rough times—I don't intend to be the one left holding
the bag, so to speak.''

"I won't change my mind," she said breathlessly.
She wanted to touch her throbbing lips with her fingertips but didn't want him to see her do it.

"Yeah, I know." His smile seemed to come more
easily, as if tensions were easing. "Your grandfather
was right about something else, too. You don't have
a clue what you're walking into. You may hate it.''

"Why would I hate it?" Unease prickled down her
spine. "What are you trying to say?''

"That you really are a babe in the woods." He
hesitated, then sat on the side of the bed. But he didn't
touch her, just clenched his hands together between
his knees. "Dara, I'll take you back to Colorado with
me if you want to go. But that's my turf, and if you
decide to come, you'll have to fit into my life, not the
other way around. If you think that'll be easy, think
again. You also have to understand I won't have either the time or the inclination to baby you.''

"I don't need or want to be babied," she said ear-
nestly. "I *am* an adult, and a complete change is exactly what I want and need. I'll pull my own
weight—you'll see!''

"Ranch life is hard," he went on relentlessly. "The
work is never done, for women as well as men. Then
when I get a minute, I take off to some rodeo or
other.''

"I'll go with you," she said quickly.

He shook his head. "Not a chance. I can't worry
about you and still concentrate on what I'm there for.

Which, in case you haven't figured it out, can get a cowboy killed.''

She *had* figured that out. She nodded unhappily. ''I know I have a lot to learn, but I'm neither weak nor foolish, despite what my grandfather believes.''

''Let's make a pact,'' he said. ''Let's not mention your grandfather again. We've got enough to worry about without that.''

''All right.'' She licked her lips. ''Uh...about the other thing...I'm sorry I asked if you were gay, but...but you confused me when you didn't...you know, you didn't...''

''I know, darlin'. Sometimes I confuse myself.''

He touched her cheek with a hand that was surprisingly gentle, then pulled back as if he regretted it. *She* didn't. His touch ignited feelings in her she'd never even dreamed about.

But he was right, she knew he was. A physical relationship between them would only complicate matters at this point. Although they were already married, their courtship lay ahead of them. She should admire his strength of character.

She *should*....

He cleared his throat. ''Okay, then, do we understand each other?''

She drew a deep, determined breath. ''Of course.''

''This is the last day of the rodeo. We'll leave for home tomorrow morning early, and I do mean *early*. It'll be just you and me, pullin' Scout in a horse trailer. Slim rode down with me, but he'd already planned to go back by way of Taos. He's got an old buddy there he likes to visit from time to time.''

"All right," she agreed. She felt so far out of her element that she'd agree to just about anything.

"I'll call home and warn—tell them I'm bringing back a wife," he said more cautiously.

"I understand." She didn't. She didn't even know how big his family was, whether it consisted of parents, brothers or sisters or all of the above.

"Fine." He stood up. "I'll call for coffee while you do whatever women do in the morning. See you in a few minutes."

Alone, she jumped out of bed and stood there trying to think about all he'd said.

And finding herself concentrating almost exclusively on that kiss.

"Jake? It's me, Zane."

His brother's voice crackled over the telephone line. "Howdy, little brother! How go the wars?"

"If you mean the rodeo wars, not worth a damn." And that didn't even begin to say it. "How's everybody?"

"Ornery as always."

"How're Kathy and the kids?"

Jake chuckled. "Kathy's fine, but those kids'll be the death of me. Missy fell off that pinto mare day before yesterday. Don't know how she managed it, but she did."

"She's only five," the indulgent uncle protested. "Did it hurt her any?"

"Nothin' hurt but her dignity. We made the mistake of laughin' at her and now she says she's through with horses—do you believe it? Kid lives on a ranch and she's through with horses.''

''She'll get over it,'' Zane said, amused by the thought of his beautiful niece stomping her little foot and laying down the law. ''And Shane?''

''They don't call 'em the terrible twos for nothin','' Jake said darkly.

Zane laughed. He adored his brother's children and considered his sister-in-law one of a kind. If he could have found a commonsense, down-to-earth girl like Kathy, he'd probably have settled down long before—

A noise behind the closed bedroom door brought reality crashing down around him. The girl he'd found was nothing like Kathy and never would be.

Jake broke into Zane's thoughts. ''So back to my original question—how's it going with you? You coming home with all the marbles?''

''I'm coming home with a wife.'' Zane just blurted it out. Jeez, could he be a little subtle?

Silence greeted his announcement. Tension tightened his scalp until he felt as if his hair were standing on end. Finally, Jake gave a tentative laugh.

''Is that some kind of joke or what?''

''It's no joke.''

''Damn! Who—what—how…? This is great, Zane. I was beginning to wonder if you'd ever settle down. Is she with you? Can I talk to her?''

''Calm down, Jake.'' Zane, sweating bullets, switched the telephone from one clammy hand to the other. ''She's taking a shower. We'll be home soon enough. I just wanted to ask if you could get the old home place ready for us.''

"That old log cabin? Why don't you move into the main house here with the rest of us? You don't want to go there, man! It's a mess. It hasn't been cleaned up since—"

"I don't care about that," Zane said, cutting his brother off. "Can you make sure we've got a fresh tank of butane and that the generator's working and the water isn't frozen? I'm not asking you to clean it up."

"But we've used it as a line camp for four or five years," Jake argued. "We're talkin' disaster. Why on earth would you take a new bride to—" He broke off abruptly. "Oh, I get it. You want privacy."

As good a reason as any, Zane realized. "You could say that."

"Even so—"

"Jake, will you just *do* it?" His patience at an end, Zane snapped out the request like an order.

"Okay, okay, don't get your spurs in a knot. Kathy and I'll go out there and do what we can."

"Dammit, I don't want you to do anything except make sure the bare necessities are available. In fact—don't even tell Kathy. There's no way in hell you could keep her from working her fingers to the bone if you did and she's got enough to do without it."

"I don't know, little brother," Jake said doubtfully. "It doesn't seem fair, takin' a new bride into something like that. Even one of our good ol' country girls would have a fainting spell walking into such a disaster. You sure she'll be okay with that kind of surprise?"

"We don't have a thing to worry about," Zane said, speaking tongue in cheek. "Mrs. Zane Farley can handle *anything*. You think I'd marry a hothouse flower?"

Without waiting for a response, he hung up the phone. Just about the only thing he *was* sure Mrs. Zane Farley could handle was *him*. And she didn't even know it.

When he'd entered the bedroom and found her all warm and pink and cuddly in the middle of that enormous bed, he'd almost lost all his careful resolve right on the spot. A cold shower had helped some, but then…but then…

Shaking with helpless laughter, he sat down on the sofa and buried his head in his hands. Gay?

Boy howdy, did she have a wrong number! He had a problem all right, but that wasn't it.

Now, he realized, it was more important than ever that he keep his wits about him. If she was going to cut and run, the sooner she did it, the better. He didn't want her hanging around until he loved her—fell in love with her and/or made love to her—before discovering that she wasn't cut out for the life of a ranch-and-rodeo wife.

Moving her into the home place, which was the original old homestead of the Farley clan, would show him right away what she was made of.

Besides smooth curves and warm skin and silken, honey-colored hair…

The bedroom door opened and Dara stood there, barefoot and swathed in a terry-cloth robe. She obviously didn't see him for she leaned over to wrap a pale pink towel around wet hair. The robe gaped open and he caught a glimpse of creamy breasts before she straightened.

Their glances locked and she started, her eyes going wide. He wondered what she saw in his face because he was fighting like hell against a purely physical response.

For a moment, neither spoke. Then she gave a nervous little laugh and tugged the robe more tightly around her.

"I thought you'd gone," she said breathlessly.

"I had a telephone call to make."

"Oh, that's right." She chewed on her full lower lip. "I...I do, too. My sister..."

"The one whose spirit your grandfather broke?"

"I only have one sister." She cocked her head, watching his expression closely. "I'm surprised you remembered that, about breaking her spirit, I mean."

"I couldn't forget it—and I sure as hell don't want it to happen to you. Your spirit's already bruised, but if I can keep it from being broken, I will."

Why had he admitted that? he berated himself. It was far too personal. Yet she seemed pleased and took a step toward him.

"So that's why you stuck with me," she said as if she'd just seen the light. She extended one slim hand in a tentative gesture.

It was the hand with the diamond ring that *hadn't* come from him. He stared at it. "That's part of my reason."

"What's the rest of it, then?"

He reached out until the tips of his fingers just

touched the tips of hers. Even that faint contact sent shock waves up his arm.

"Zane," she said again, "what's the rest of the reason we're here together?"

With a superhuman effort, he dropped his hand. "I honestly don't know," he said in a flat voice.

Since it was a lie, he didn't hang around to debate it with her. He knew why. He wanted her. If he could ever be sure of her... But that seemed unlikely, considering the way they'd gotten together.

The hell with it. He had places to go and people to see.

"Blythe, it's me, Dara."

"Dara, honey! I didn't expect to hear from you while you're on your honeymoon."

"About that..."

Blythe chuckled. "So how's Blake, or need I ask?"

"You can ask, but I can't answer. He's not here."

"He's not...? Did he step out for something?"

"He stepped out for good. Grandfather got to him."

Blythe's entire tone changed. "Oh, no! Are you all right? I'm sorry I mentioned honeymoon. I had no idea—"

"But I am on my honeymoon. That's what I called to tell you...."

While she sketched an abbreviated version of what had happened, Dara thought about her sister. Blythe was thirty-one now and completely dependent upon their grandfather for her entire life. Dara felt her own resolve stiffen even more.

"So that's the gist of it, Blythe," she concluded. "My cowboy is handsome and brave and strong, and Grandfather couldn't back him down an inch."

"But you don't know him! Oh, Dara, I'm afraid for you."

"You knew Trevor for almost a year and it didn't do you any good. Honey, one of Zane's friends said it was fate and I...I think it must be."

There was a moment of silence and then Blythe whispered, "I hear something in your voice. Are you in *love* with him already, Dara?"

Dara's heart leaped. "I...I don't know. Maybe— but speaking rationally, I know that's crazy. At the very least, I think he's the most wonderful man I've ever met. When Grandfather pulled out his check- book—"

"He didn't! Right in front of you?"

"He did. Zane was so offended I thought he'd punch Grandfather in the nose. Blythe, he's taking me back to his ranch in Colorado. Isn't that incredibly romantic? He's a big important cattleman and I'll han- dle all his entertaining, plan the most fabulous par- ties—"

"Of course you will, dear."

Dara heard the sob in her sister's voice and remorse flooded through her. "I'm sorry, Blythe," she said miserably. "It must seem as if I'm about to desert you, but I've got to get away from Grandfather before I do something really drastic."

She caught her breath. She'd made it worse. She might as well have added, "before I end up like you."

Of course, Blythe understood anyway. "I'm happy

for you,'' she declared, her voice gaining strength. ''You're right to take a chance. I took a chance and lost, but mine was a foolish chance with a man I thought I knew but didn't. How much worse can it be your way?''

How much worse indeed? Following a flurry of goodbyes and we'll-talk-soons, Dara hung up the receiver. For a long time, she stood there alone in the bedroom with her hand still on the telephone and her thoughts in turmoil.

Then she took a deep breath and went in search of the stranger who was her husband, even if in name only.

CHAPTER SEVEN

DARA and Zane didn't head out of Las Vegas at dawn the next day. To Dara's astonished horror, they headed out well *before* dawn. He roused her out of bed at who-knew-what ungodly hour, grabbed her suitcases and herded her out of the luxurious MGM Grand Hotel before she even had time to put on her makeup.

With her soft leather jacket draped across her shoulders, she promptly fell asleep in the corner of his enormous pickup truck almost as soon as he hustled her inside. Only a few minutes later, the pickup stopped; she sensed activity, felt the vehicle lurch and never even opened her eyes.

Dara was not a morning person and the sooner he realized it, the better. With her arm cradling her head, she sank deeper into dreamland.

When she awakened, she didn't know where she was. Sitting up straight, she looked around groggily. The first thing she saw was Zane behind the wheel, grinning at her. He looked alert and vital and very, *very* attractive.

"Good mornin', sunshine," he said in a warm, husky voice.

She groaned and pushed tangled hair away from her face. "Are you sure?"

"Hey, look around. It's a beautiful day."

She followed his advice and what she saw—gray skies, scrubby brush and trees with barren limbs—fell a little short of "beautiful". She swallowed hard. "This isn't how I thought Nevada would look," she admitted.

"Just as well," he said with perfect seriousness, "since we're in Utah."

"Utah! But what happened to Nevada?"

"It's back there," he assured her. "Las Vegas is only an hour or so from the border with Arizona."

"Arizona!" She slumped on the bench seat. "Then what are we doing in Utah? Did I miss an entire state?"

He laughed out loud. "I take it from your reaction that your grasp of geography is a little on the weak side," he said when his mirth subsided.

"I guess you could draw that conclusion," she admitted. "I've never been in this part of the country before, at least on the ground. I've flown over it on the way to someplace else."

"Then this should be a real treat for you," he said. "We don't call it God's Country for nothing."

"I'll take your word for it." She swallowed to ease her dry mouth and throat. "Uh…you wouldn't have anything around to drink?"

"Coffee in that thermos by your feet." He nodded toward the floorboard. "And there's a few doughnuts in that box between us on the seat."

She shuddered. "I don't do doughnuts." She set about opening the thermos. Seeing no other cup, she poured the steaming liquid into the plastic lid. "Sugar? Cream?"

He gave her an incredulous glance. "Get outta here!"

"Sorry." She sipped and burned her tongue, but it was worth it. As the coffee warmed her stomach, she began to feel almost human. "So," she tried again, "we're in Utah, heading…?"

"Cattywampus across the whole durn state."

"Catty…?"

"We came in at the southwest corner and we'll cross the state and come out in the middle of the eastern border with Colorado. But that'll take a while. Right now we're on Highway 15 heading for the junction with Highway 70. Seventy'll take us almost all the way to Faraway, which is this side of Denver in the mountains."

"Oh." She said it rather forlornly as the true depth of her ignorance sank in. "When will we get there?"

"Depends. If we were in a car, it'd only take us eleven or twelve hours. Old Scout back there'll slow us down some."

"Scout?" His horse! She shifted in the seat, not easy to manage with a seat belt on, and looked behind. Sure enough, a silver-and-black trailer followed. She also saw her luggage next to his in the pickup bed.

"Gotta stop every once in a while and let Scout stretch his legs," Zane explained. "You, too, most likely. I gather you're not used to this kind of travel."

"No." She added quickly, "But I'm willing to learn."

"Probably won't be any need." He glanced at the dashboard. "We'll stop up here a ways at Salina, get some gas and unload Scout for a few minutes. Maybe you can get something to eat.'' The corner of his mouth, in profile, tilted. ''Although I don't know what you've got against doughnuts. To cowboys they're practically health food.''

She made a face. ''Grandfather wouldn't even let them in the house. He never believed in indulging children, or anyone else for that matter.''

''Well, I think I'll indulge myself with one of the chocolate-frosted variety, if you'll pull it out for me.''

''Sure.'' She placed the box on her lap and opened the flap. The sweet smell of chocolate assaulted her nostrils and she sucked in a deep, appreciative breath. She adored chocolate but rarely allowed herself to indulge. Picking up a doughnut, she offered it to him.

He took it and his hand brushed hers. Starting back, she instinctively thrust her fingers into her mouth. The smooth, seductive taste of chocolate flooded her senses.

She groaned. ''Maybe just one.'' She reached into the box.

Zane swallowed his doughnut in a few bites. As if mesmerized, she watched him follow her lead and lick chocolate off his fingers. Her mouth went dry.

He turned his head toward her. ''Think I can have a sip of that coffee?''

''Oh, of course. But we've only got the one cup. Just let me…'' She struggled to roll down the window to toss out what remained in the cup so she could pour more for him.

He stopped her with a hand on her arm. ''Don't be silly. We can drink from the same cup.''

And live in the same house and eat from the same

table and sleep in the same bed? she wondered a bit wildly. It seemed so intimate to offer him her cup and watch him put his lips where hers had rested.

He finished drinking and handed back the cup. "Thanks."

A chocolate smudge decorated the edge of his mouth, and without thinking, she reached out with her thumb to wipe it away with a quick motion.

When he'd touched her hand, she'd all but flinched. When she touched his cheek, his eyelashes fluttered in reaction, but he didn't move a muscle.

She gave him a self-conscious smile. "You had chocolate on your face," she explained breathlessly.

"I figured." With a half smile, he turned his full attention toward the road ahead. "Next stop, Salina, Utah."

Zane explained what they were seeing as they progressed across Utah and through Colorado's back door. Highway 70 followed a route through the high desert, he said, pointing out farms and cattle ranges. As they moved into the mountains, the views of valley and plateau became breathtaking to a girl from the Pacific coast.

They crossed into Colorado just below Grand Junction, stopping long enough to walk Scout and pick up a bag of hamburgers. Grandfather would have a heart attack if he knew, Dara thought happily and without a trace of guilt. From that point on, they were *really* in the mountains.

Awed by towering, snowcapped peaks and rushing rivers, Dara found herself becoming more and more enchanted with the land that would be her new home—and enchanted with her handsome husband-in-name-only who'd brought her here. Even the names of the towns delighted her, names like Parachute, Rifle, Silt.

Zane drove fast but with consummate skill. The highway was smooth and wide in addition to being mountainous and often curving. When she finally worked up her nerve to offer to drive so he could rest, he thanked her brusquely and declined.

Since she had no experience driving pickups or hauling horse trailers, she drew a relieved breath. But she'd have tried, she assured herself; she really would have tried her best to help him in any way she could.

The day passed with stops only for gas and junk food and to "stretch old Scout's legs." The scenery, although still awesome, became a blur of evergreens and rocks and steep slopes. Zane spoke only occasionally, about the scenery mostly. Dara wanted desperately to question him about his family but felt tongue-tied at the possibility of annoying him with probing questions. After a few cautious attempts at conversation, she fell silent, letting him set the conversational tone.

As dark fell, so did she—asleep in her corner of the cab.

When she awoke again, she'd lost all track of time. The pickup and trailer moved smoothly through utter darkness; it could be eight o'clock or midnight. Since it didn't much matter which, she didn't bother to ask.

Zane glanced at her, his expression revealed in the green glow from the instrument panel. "Feel better?"

"I didn't feel bad before," she objected. She stifled a yawn. "I don't know why I was so tired."

"It gets monotonous just goin' on down the road," he said. "At least when you're driving, you've got a reason to concentrate." He flexed his shoulders beneath the plaid shirt.

"You must be tired," she said, feeling suddenly guilty. "You've been driving for hours."

"I'm used to it," he said. "When I'm on the circuit—"

"Circuit?"

"Rodeo circuit. Normally, that's the Mountain States Circuit. See, the circuit system has twelve geographic regions. The Mountain States Circuit is one of 'em and includes Colorado and Wyoming. It's…complicated unless you're used to it. Anyway, I'm used to throwing old Scout in the trailer and taking off at a moment's notice. This is a longer haul than most, but I've done it enough that it's no big deal."

"That makes me feel a *little* better," she conceded, trying to stretch her legs a little. "So where are we headed exactly, and when will we get there?"

"We're heading for my family's old home place," he said, taking an off-ramp and exiting the freeway. "I thought that might be a better place for us to get to…well, to get to know each other. If we moved in with the family, we wouldn't have a minute's peace."

Her stomach clenched. *Get to know each other…* She swallowed hard before going on. "You haven't said much about your family."

"What's the point? You'll make up your own mind when you meet them."

"I suppose. Uh…just what is an 'old home place'?"

Her question elicited a laugh. "Just that. The first Farley in these parts built his home there. It started as a one-room log cabin, and over the years since, Farleys added on to it. Eventually, it made more sense to build a new house closer to the road instead of building the road to the old place. For the past thirty years, the old place has been used by ranch workers and for storage."

A cold chill passed down Dara's backbone. Nobody had really lived there for thirty years? What was she walking into?

The road they traveled became narrower, bumpier. Zane slowed, then turned again, slowed even more. Where the lights aimed, Dara saw snow and it made her cold even to look at it. She had almost no experience with snow. She'd been to Big Bear, a mountain in southern California, only once. She'd enjoyed fifteen or twenty minutes of snowballs and snow angels before hurrying back down to sunshine and balmy temperatures.

That was about it, which wasn't *nearly* enough to prepare her for this.

Zane braked the pickup and pointed toward the shape revealed by the vehicle's headlights. "We're here," he said with a satisfaction so deep she could feel it. "Welcome to your new home, Dara."

If she hadn't already been sitting down, she'd have keeled over.

*   *   *

Zane worked hard to keep from laughing out loud.

If he'd ever seen a woman flummoxed, this was the one. She stared at the cabin as if it were a shack in Dogpatch. Then she swallowed hard and said bravely, "It looks…very interesting."

It sure did. Even Zane, who knew and loved every log and nail in the primitive construction, had to agree with that.

"Come on," he ordered. Grabbing a flashlight from beneath the seat, he threw open his door. "I'll take you inside before I see to Scout." The horse was impatient, banging his rear hooves against the trailer door, but he'd just have to wait.

Dara scrambled after him, the heels of her pumps sinking into the snow. She made a soft little sound of protest but didn't complain, just floundered forward beside him. Then she stepped into a hole and sank into snow up to the knees of her fancy tailored slacks.

Without further ado, Zane picked her up in his arms and carried her the rest of the way to the porch. She gasped and clung to him and he caught the aroma of wildflowers in the silky blond curls tickling his face.

She felt almost fragile in his arms, although he hadn't thought of her like that before. Perhaps it was the way she clung to him, her leather jacket crushed between them. Perhaps it was the soft, moist feel of her breath on his throat when she whispered his name.

"Zane," she gasped, "this is silly. You must be exhausted. I can walk."

"I know you can."

He carried her up the broad front steps and paused at the door only long enough to give it a good shot with one booted foot. It swung open instantly, as he'd expected it would.

"Didn't you ever hear of a bride being carried over the threshold?" he teased. Hoisting her to an easier hold, he let the beam of light drop until it touched the floor, then carried her across the threshold. Still holding her, he kicked the door closed and turned back. "Can you reach the light switch next to the door?" he asked. "It's right there somewhere...."

She leaned toward the wall and blinding light suddenly filled the room. He blinked at the shock of it and lowered her to her feet.

"Here it is," he said with soft satisfaction. "Your new home." Putting his hands on her shoulders, he turned her slowly around.

If the outside had shocked her, the inside stunned her. They stood in a good-sized room, but that was the only good thing that could be said. The other word that sprang to mind was "disaster".

The place was a mess. Trash lay everywhere. Cans and papers and discarded boxes and packages littered the floor. A layer of dust and cobwebs and more junk tumbled over the furniture, most of which looked handmade and older than time. The whole sorry mess was just a heart-stopping hodgepodge of misuse and abuse.

Zane glanced at her and his guarded expression turned into a frown. "I guess it does look kinda bad," he conceded, "but we'll get it all cleaned up tomorrow. Wonder if the kitchen's any better."

The kitchen? A horrible realization swept over her;

she'd be expected to use a kitchen. Obviously, she wasn't going to have outside help in a little ramshackle place like this. Her grandfather's domestics would turn up their noses at such a suggestion.

He cocked his head. "Are you hungry? I don't think we'll find anything here, but we've still got a couple of hamburgers in the truck from that last stop."

She'd rather starve than face another hamburger. "I think I'm more tired than hungry," she said truthfully. "My bedroom is…where?"

"There." He pointed to one of two doors leading from the far side of the room. "There's *only* one, so you can't get lost. The other door's the bathroom and the kitchen's through that doorway over there."

Whistling cheerfully, he turned back outside to take care of Scout while his bride tried to face the enormity of her disappointment. This was *not* how she'd expected a big Colorado rancher to live!

"Hey, wake up, sleepyhead!"

Dara tried to ignore whatever was trying to shake her out of warm and fuzzy dreams. She was lounging beside an Olympic-size swimming pool next to a ranch house only slightly bigger than that of the Ewings in the old television show called "Dallas". Uniformed servants carried trays of frosty drinks…

Or perhaps it wasn't the drinks that were frosty. Tugging at the covers threatening to slip away, she groaned and kept her eyes squeezed tightly shut.

Their arrival last night had been a bad dream—a

nightmare. If she could just resist opening her eyes, maybe everything would right itself.

"Okay," Zane's voice pummeled her determination, "but I thought you'd want to meet the family. Guess I'll just have to tell 'em you're—"

"What?" Bolting upright in the bed, she stared at him through blurry eyes. "Your family's here?"

"Comin'," he said. "Saw their exhaust trail turn off the main road. "You've got ten, maybe fifteen minutes to pull yourself together."

It would take a lot longer than that, she feared, sprinting into the bathroom and flinging herself beneath the cold spray of a shower that took its own sweet time heating up. In fact, the way she felt now, she might never get her wits together again.

She couldn't believe she'd fallen asleep before Zane even returned to the house last night, but she had. And she'd slept like a log all night long without any idea where *he'd* slept. Not with her, surely; she'd have known if he'd crawled into bed with her. But where would he sleep tonight?

Shivering, she slipped into wool slacks and a cashmere sweater, then combed her wet hair into a ponytail. Sliding her feet into handmade suede loafers, she took a deep breath and hurried into the living room.

She stopped short at the sight that greeted her astonished eyes: Zane, holding a small boy while a girl of perhaps five hugged his waist and looked up at him with a delighted smile on her freckled face. A man and a woman stood by, grinning with obvious approval.

And then they saw Dara and the grins disappeared as if removed with an eraser from a chalkboard. Dara felt her own smile slip away in response. My goodness, what had they expected? Or judging from their expressions, maybe the question was *whom* had they expected?

The woman recovered first. Stepping forward, she thrust out her hand. "Hi," she said brightly. She was dressed just like the man, in jeans and boots and sheepskin-lined jacket, her cheeks glowing red with the sting of cold air. "I'm Zane's sister-in-law, Kathy."

Dara's answering smile felt shaky. "I'm Dara Lin—I mean Farley." She felt herself blushing. "I'm so happy to meet you."

"And I'm happy to meet you," Kathy said heartily. "If Zane's not going to do the honors…" She glanced at her brother-in-law with affection.

"You're doin' fine," Zane drawled. "Be my guest."

"I'll do that. Dara, I'd like you to meet my husband, Jake, who also happens to be your brother-in-law." She indicated the man standing there with his jaw hanging down. "He normally shows better manners," she added tartly.

Jake, who looked like a young version of the Marlboro man and an older version of Zane, stepped forward. "Welcome to the Farley family, such as it is," he declared. "Don't know how you got tangled up with this no-account brother of mine, but you roped him and tied him in record time and that's good enough for me."

Dara, a step behind him all through that sentence, smiled a bit uncertainly. "There's only one roper in this family and it certainly isn't me."

Jake laughed. "You got me on that one. Since Kathy didn't mention it, I'll add that those two kids playing over there with the rope belong to us. We all want to welcome you to the Bar F—Dara, is it?"

"That's right. And I'm happy to be here."

"If that's the truth," Kathy jumped in, "you're a brave woman. This place is a mess!" She shook her head and pursed her lips. "I don't know why Jake waited until this morning to tell me Zane had called and said he'd gotten married and was bringin' his new wife here. I certainly would have come over and tried to clean up a little if I'd known. Oh, well, I'm here now."

"But..." Dara spared a glance at Zane. He was busy with the children—perhaps too busy, she thought darkly. Apparently, he wanted her to sink or swim with his family all by herself.

She'd be damned if she'd go down without a struggle. Lifting her chin, she smiled at her new relations.

"There'll be plenty of time to clean up later," she said firmly. "At the moment, I could do with a hot cup of *anything* and I'll bet the rest of you feel the same. Maybe somebody left some coffee or tea behind." She draped a friendly arm over her new sister-in-law's shoulder and turned her toward the doorway. "I haven't even been inside the kitchen yet," she confessed. "It was so late when we got here last night and Zane pulled me bodily out of bed only minutes before you arrived."

"Danged fool," Jake muttered under his breath with an amused glance at his brother. "Bet you'll never make *that* mistake again."

Dara leaped to her husband's defense. "Oh, but if he hadn't, who knows when I might have decided to drag myself out..."

And then she realized that Jake hadn't been commenting on the state of her exhaustion—or if he was, he attributed that exhaustion to an entirely different source.

She was, after all, a brand-new bride.

If they only knew!

CHAPTER EIGHT

IT WASN'T easy but eventually Dara found the coffee, the coffeepot and—in Kathy—someone willing to tell her how to use both. Feeling foolish, she frowned at the battered metal pot perking away happily on the old-fashioned gas cookstove.

"One problem solved." Dara looked around the kitchen, feeling helpless, as well. "Where...where do you think I might look for the cups?"

Kathy burst into laughter. "I'm not laughing at you," she said quickly. "It's just that you're...well, you're the *lostest*-looking little thing I've ever seen in my life."

Dara groaned. "That's what Slim said the first time *he* saw me and then he insisted on introducing me to his friends. Look how that turned out!"

"So Slim Sanders introduced you and Zane, did he?" Kathy dug through the pile of dirty dishes in the sink, triumphantly pulling out a battered tin cup.

"Yes. I guess he recognized a damsel in distress when he saw one."

Kathy's glance betrayed her curiosity. "I hope you'll share all that with me someday, but at the moment..." She reached down into the sink again and came up with another cup, which she held out triumphantly. "Now all we've got to do is find two

115

more!''

And together, they did.

Zane leaned against the kitchen doorway drinking coffee and watching Dara—his wife, although he still had trouble with that concept—at the table with Missy. The blue-eyed, brown-haired little girl was talking a mile a minute. Dara listened with perfect concentration. Jake had gone outside to take a look at the corral—he thought it probably needed some work—but he'd made a point of leaving Zane inside with the women.

A light touch on his elbow brought Zane swinging around. Kathy stood there. Although she was about the same size as Dara, the two women couldn't have looked more different. With her brown hair and freckles and wide-open smile, Kathy seemed much the more confident of the two.

At the moment, she wasn't smiling. She gestured him into the living room with a crooked finger. He sighed. He hated having Kathy on his case.

''Now, don't get started,'' he said in a warning tone.

''I'm already started.'' She gave an indignant sniff. ''Zane Farley, when Jake said you were married, I naturally assumed you and Jody—''

''You assumed wrong.''

Her smile was a surprise to him. ''I'm glad. Dara's really…sweet. She's way out of her element, but she's going to be all right.''

He felt somewhat less optimistic. ''We'll see, I guess. The sooner the better.…''

Kathy's head jerked back. ''Are you expecting

Dara to get fed up fast and run? Just because your mother—''

''We won't talk about my mother,'' he interrupted, his voice cold where before it had been humorously indulgent. ''But if Dara does decide to take off, she won't be leavin' any kids behind.''

Kathy was silent for a moment and then she nodded. ''I see your point, but I think you've got her all wrong. Which makes me wonder how in the world you two got together in the first place.''

Zane shrugged, but her speculative tone made him uneasy. He'd known his sudden marriage would raise talk. He'd avoided tying the knot for so long that he knew many people, family members among them, had begun to wonder if any woman would ever trip him up.

He'd wondered himself. And then Dara Linnell had walked into the Golden Gringo in Las Vegas and changed his life forever. But she wasn't going to change *him*, and she wasn't going to slip around the defenses he'd built over the years since his mother walked.

When Dara went, she wouldn't leave anything behind, including broken hearts. He'd damned well make sure of that.

Even five-year-old Missy knows more about cleaning than I do, Dara thought with disgust. Still, the two of them had managed to do a credible job on the kitchen while Kathy tackled the rest of the cabin. In the process, Dara had discovered that the cupboard wasn't entirely bare. She could at least offer her new husband and his family a sandwich lunch.

Hand in hand with the ebullient Missy, Dara went in search of Kathy, expecting to find her in the bedroom. Instead, she found Zane, sitting on the neatly made bed and staring past the open closet door with a stunned expression on his face.

She stopped short at the sight of him, but Missy rushed forward to throw her arms around her uncle's neck. ''Whatcha doin', Uncle Zane?'' she wanted to know. ''Where's Mama and my brother?''

''Your mama went out to the barn to talk to your daddy and took Shane with her.''

''Can I go, too? Can I?'' The little girl looked from one adult to another for permission.

''Sure,'' Zane agreed. He glanced quickly at Dara. ''That is, unless you—''

''No, that's fine,'' she said quickly.

''Thanks, Aunt Dara!'' Missy skipped the few steps to the door, gave Dara a quick hug and skipped out.

Dara stared at Zane, feeling a warm glow. How easily the little girl accepted her into the family. How easily Missy's parents accepted their new sister-in-law. Now if only Zane…

She frowned. He looked so…puzzled. ''What is it?'' she wanted to know.

''It's those *clothes*.'' He gestured helplessly.

Dismayed, she stared at the open closet. Her few things hung next to Zane's and she realized with a start that her underwear probably shared a drawer with his. Kathy had unpacked.

This was *their* bedroom, not hers. A little shiver of

anticipation shot up her spine. They'd also be sharing the single bath and the meals she would be expected to cook.

"Zane," she said hesitantly, "that's hardly anything, just what I could get into one suitcase."

"But a little fancy for around here. I'll have to take you into Faraway to pick up a few things before we get our next big snow or you'll be in trouble."

Feeling despondent, she sat down on the end of the bed, careful not to infringe upon his space. Instead of looking at him, she stared down at her hands in her lap. "That may be the least of the trouble I'm in," she said.

"Which means what?"

She sighed. "You may have noticed that I'm not terribly good at cleaning?"

"Uh...I did sense a certain...lack of expertise. But if I'm not worried, why should you be?" He sounded amused.

She wasn't. "I clean better than I cook," she informed him darkly.

"Can you read?"

"Quite well." Finally, Dara thought, something I'm actually good at.

"Then you can cook," Zane said. "I've heard Kathy tell Missy a hundred times, if you can read, you can cook."

She felt the mattress shift beneath his weight and supposed he was about to leave the room, but instead she felt his hands settle on her shoulders. She tensed in response but didn't try to pull away.

"Relax."

The word was a warm murmur directly behind her right ear and she shivered. With strong sure fingers, he began to knead the tight muscles beneath the soft yarn of her sweater.

He made an exclamation of surprise and probed with his thumbs. "You're really tense," he said in a husky voice. "Let go, Dara. You're doing great. The Farleys aren't near as dangerous as they look."

Only one Farley struck her as being the least bit dangerous and that was the one manipulating her tight muscles. She felt one kind of tension flowing away only to be replaced with another...more hazardous kind. His touch was sheer magic.

"We'll get you a cookbook and you'll do fine."

"You've got more confidence in me than I do in myself." She couldn't breathe and every muscle felt as if it had turned into liquid fire. He slid his hands lower along her spine and she arched like a cat.

"That's because I know something you don't. The Farley men aren't exactly sophisticated eaters." His chuckle warmed her. "Meat and potatoes and plenty of 'em and I'm happy." He gave her shoulder a final pat and stood up. "Don't worry. I'm not hard to please and I give points for trying."

Kathy's embarrassed voice was a shock to Dara's already overloaded nervous system. "*Oh, excuse me! I didn't know—*"

"No problem," Zane said. "I was just on my way out to the barn." He saluted the two women with the fingers of one hand and walked through the doorway, quickly vacated by Kathy and Missy.

"I'm so sorry!" Kathy put a restraining hand on her daughter's shoulder.

"About what?" Cheeks warm, Dara smoothed the sweater around her waist and tried to even out her breathing.

"I interrupted something."

"Not really. I was just telling Zane I can't cook."

Kathy gave a wry giggle. "I sincerely doubt Zane married you for your cooking."

Dara rolled her eyes heavenward. "You'd be surprised if you knew why Zane married me," she said gloomily, "you really would. Maybe someday, if I get desperate enough, I'll tell you all about it. In the meantime—Missy, how are you with peanut butter sandwiches?"

Fortunately, Missy turned out to be a whiz.

Zane and Dara followed the Farleys out to their vehicle to say goodbye. "I'll drop by tomorrow to bring you a few things you'll need around here," Kathy called, waving through an open window despite the chill in the air. "And we'll talk about Christmas—it's only a little more than a week away!"

"Christmas!" Dara felt genuine dismay as she watched the pickup drive away. She shivered, hugging her arms around her waist. The delicate knit of her sweater did little to protect her from the sharp wind blowing off the mountains.

Zane slid an arm around her shoulders and turned her toward the house. She felt instantly warmer, protected.

"Don't worry about the holidays," he advised,

bending his head against the wind and leading her up the steps and into the house. "I picked up a couple of things for the kids while I was in Las Vegas and they can be from both of us."

"But—"

"There's no time, Dara." Releasing her, he gestured around the room, which looked better than when they'd arrived last night but nowhere near *good*. "We've already got our hands full."

"All right, Zane." Giving in was second nature to her. She always gave in when her grandfather used that tone on her—or had until recently. But she couldn't help feeling disappointed.

Zane reached for his jacket hanging on a coatrack near the door.

"Where are you going?" she asked with quick alarm.

"I've got as much to do outside as you have to do inside." He buttoned the jacket up to his chin. "Talked to Jake. He figures he can spare Slim, so he'll be movin' into the bunkhouse soon as he gets back from Taos. We'll be moving some stock over here for the winter, along with a few horses. I'll need to check fence, shore up the corral, clean up the barn…"

She plucked his hat from the rack before he could do it himself and rose on tiptoe to place it on his head. Trying to hide her disappointment, she smiled. "All right. When will you be back?"

He grinned, straight white teeth flashing. "In time for supper. Say six o'clock?"

Supper. Oh dear. "Of course."

He hesitated and something in his expression seemed to soften. "You did good, Dara."

She blinked. "At what?"

"At meeting a whole herd of strangers on strange turf. They all liked you."

"Did they?" That possibility filled her heart with gladness. "I liked them, too."

He smiled. "I was proud of you."

Her heart soared. But before she could think how to respond, he was gone, leaving behind nothing but a blast of cold air…and one warm memory.

The fried potatoes were more than half-raw and the beef was overdone to the point of shoe leather, but Zane ate them without a word of complaint.

Dara tried to do the same but found it impossible. "This is awful!" She put down the knife with which she'd been sawing the meat on her plate. "I don't know what went wrong."

"Don't worry about it." He grinned. "I told you I wasn't picky. Besides, you'll get better—won't you?"

"I hope so!" She rolled her eyes.

"In the meantime, I won't starve. *You* may—" he glanced at her full plate "—but I definitely won't. So it's not apple pie à la mode—"

"Is that your favorite?"

He looked startled. "Yeah, I guess so. But believe me, I don't expect you to start whipping out pies in your spare time." He glanced around the kitchen. "Place is lookin' better already."

"Thank you. I'm trying." She dropped raw red hands into her lap to hide them.

"I can see that."

Reaching over, he lifted one of her hands and held it in his. With gentle deliberation, he soothed the knuckle she'd scraped with the potato peeler. His touch both comforted and excited her.

"I do have a question, though," she said in a voice that trembled.

"Shoot." He replaced her hand in her lap, then leaned back in his chair and gave her his full attention.

She felt bereft but plunged ahead. "I didn't find a telephone."

He raised dark brows and one corner of his mouth quirked in a near smile. "Never had one installed. This place is the end of the road—literally. Never seemed worth the trouble or expense."

"No television, either?"

"Nope. We don't have time for television out here." Clearly, this amused him. "We do have books, though."

She nodded solemnly. "I found them. Lots of cowboy books along with a few horse books and a cow book or two for variety."

His big grin broke though. "We'll be going into town tomorrow or the next day to pick up a few things for you. We'll make sure that includes a supply of books. Now…" He stood. "I've got a saddle that needs repairing out in the barn. You can go on to bed whenever it suits you."

Lips parted, she stared at him, hurt by what felt like a dismissal. She had thought he enjoyed talking to her, soothing her small hurts. And they still had so much they needed to discuss....

When she didn't ask the obvious, he volunteered it. "I'll be sleeping out here on the sofa for the time being. There's a lot to be settled between us before we start sharin' a bed."

She couldn't help asking, "Such as?"

"Such as whether or not we've got a future together. If we don't, we ought to find it out before we do anything…rash."

Rash, as in making love, she translated. She felt somehow rejected by his attitude, even realizing he was entirely correct—if they were going to be sensible. Without a commitment, heartache seemed inevitable.

She watched him leave, trying to convince herself she was relieved.

In town the following day, Dara got the shock of her life. When she offered her charge card to pay for a stack of books she'd chosen as Christmas gifts for the Farleys, the clerk came back with an embarrassed expression.

"I'm sorry," the young woman said, "but this card has been declined. I'll have to confiscate it for return to the company."

"But that's impossible!" Dara stared at the clerk. "There must be some mistake." But then she knew there wasn't any mistake; her grandfather had done this to her. Seething, she fought to control her temper. "May I use your telephone to make a collect call?"

"I'm sorry, but there's this policy…" The young woman looked sympathetic. "Oh, what the heck! Just be sure to make it collect." She winked, then turned her back and strolled casually to the opposite side of the small bookstore.

Dara dialed her grandfather's office with trembling fingers. When she identified herself, his secretary put her through immediately.

"Princess! Where are you calling from?"

"A little town in Colorado, not that it matters."

"Oh." That single word conveyed a wealth of disappointment. "I thought perhaps—"

"I know what you thought. Grandfather, why did you cancel my charge card?"

"Because you can no longer pay the bills."

"Of course I can! I had twenty-seven thousand dollars in my checking account the last time I looked."

"Look again, sweetheart. That's frozen now."

"You can't do this to me!" she cried, her heart beginning to pound in her chest. She had counted on that money for...for a sort of dowry. She couldn't come to Zane without a penny to her name, beyond the few dollars in her wallet.

"I can and I have," Donald Linnell said, his voice matter-of-fact. "I told you how it would be if you persevered in this ill-conceived marriage." His voice grew almost contemptuous. "So how is the cowboy?"

"My husband is fine," she yelled at him, "and if you think this is going to make me come crawling back—"

A big hand reached over her shoulder, took the telephone receiver from her hand and replaced it gently on the cradle. Whirling, she found Zane standing there with a grim expression on his handsome face.

"I take it your grandpa's cut off your credit."

"Yes, and it's totally unfair. He's also frozen my bank account."

"That doesn't matter."

"Of course it matters! I'm penniless. I have little more than the clothes on my back."

"Then we'll have to do something about that." Taking her elbow in an unyielding hand, he steered her toward the door. "Stacy," he called to the clerk still on the other side of the store, "wrap up these things for my wife and put them on my card. We'll be back to pick everything up in a half hour or so."

"Sure thing, Zane. Sorry about that, but I didn't know she was your—"

Zane let the door slam closed on the rest of the clerk's incredulity.

Zane bought Dara a hat, boots, jeans and a heavy winter jacket. He wanted to buy her more—several shirts caught his eye as well as a wide, tooled leather belt with a turquoise-studded buckle. But Dara was too embarrassed to let him do more than the absolute minimum.

Even then, she felt like a charity case. She didn't like depending upon someone she barely knew for money. She'd never imagined how it would make her feel to know someone else would pay the bill, even someone as generous as this new husband of hers.

To his credit, Zane seemed cool about the situation. With everything stowed in the pickup, they drove back to the home place in silence, just as big fat snowflakes began to fall.

A red pickup was parked in front. When they entered the cabin with their arms full of packages, Kathy looked up with a smile from her seat on the sofa. Shane sat at her feet, playing with a handful of miniature cars. He, too, paused long enough to smile.

"Hi, all," Kathy said cheerfully. "Hope you don't mind me coming on in."

"You have a key?" Dara dropped her packages on the sofa.

"That door's never locked." Kathy looked amused. "I see you two have been shopping."

"Yeah," Zane said, "and now I've got to get out to the barn to see if that roof's gonna hold if we get as much snow as it looks like we might."

Dara watched him go, then sighed and let her shoulders droop.

Kathy stood up. "What is it, honey?"

"N-nothing—yes, something!" Slipping out of her jacket, Dara tossed it onto the coatrack. "I just found out that my grandfather has canceled my charge card and frozen my checking account. I'm destitute." She gestured to the packages. "Zane had to pay for all these things and it's humiliating!"

"Oh, my goodness! Do you have a lot to learn about being married!"

Drawn by the amusement in Kathy's voice, Dara gave her new friend a puzzled glance. "Well, I know *that!* And I have a lot to learn about cooking and cleaning and just about everything else worth doing or knowing. But I don't see why Zane should have to spend *his* money—"

"Not his money, *your* money, in the plural. The

two of you are a couple now. What's his is also yours.''

"And what's mine is nonexistent, so what's he getting out of this deal? It just isn't fair.'' Dara shook her head. "I don't want to sponge off him.''

Kathy looked shocked. "Sponge off him! That's not what's going on. You ask what Zane's getting out of this and I'll tell you. He's getting a wife who loves him.'' She pointed this out as if it was only obvious. "And you're getting a husband who loves you. The jeans and boots he bought you—''

"How'd you know what he bought me?''

"Honey, I know what you needed. But whatever he bought you, that isn't what's important in this marriage. Love is.''

"Oh, if only—''

"None of that now. You're just down in the dumps because of what happened in town. Zane loves you or he'd never have married you. I *know* him—I know *all* the Farleys.''

"Kathy, you *don't*.'' Dara took the other woman's hands in a crushing grip and stared pleadingly into her eyes. "The way it happened—''

"I don't want you to tell me anything you'll regret,'' Kathy interrupted, shaking her head for emphasis. "I've known Zane Farley all his life. I'd have sworn he didn't believe in marriage and wouldn't commit to one woman if somebody held a gun to his head—or I would have, right up to the minute I met you.''

Leaning forward, Kathy gave Dara a light kiss on the cheek. "I *would* like to know what happened in

Las Vegas, though, and someday when the time is right... But not now.'' All business, she added, ''I brought you a cookbook and some cleaning supplies you'll be needing around here. Go ahead and put your packages away while I go get everything. Shane, you stay there and Mama will be right back.''

The dark-eyed little boy glanced calmly at his mother, then turned his attention back to the little red sports car clutched in his chubby fist.

For a moment, Dara stood there, praying that everything Kathy had said was true...but knowing it couldn't be. Then with a sigh, she scooped up the packages and carried them into the bedroom.

CHAPTER NINE

DARA thought the man must surely be made of steel. As the days passed and they continued living together in the little log cabin, she felt her resistance—what little she'd ever felt where he was concerned—eroding further. He, on the other hand, seemed entirely oblivious to her feelings—and to have none at all of his own!

She'd never imagined how intimate it would be to live with a man in such constricted quarters. The first time she walked out of the bedroom and found him shaving with the bathroom door wide open, she'd had to stop and stare.

It was such an ordinary masculine chore, and yet she couldn't recall ever seeing the ritual performed before. Wearing only his usual Wranglers low on his hips, he leaned forward to peer into the cracked mirror of the medicine cabinet.

Suddenly, he yelped and jumped back. A tiny dot of blood marred the perfect whiteness of his lathered chin.

She gasped. "Oh, my goodness, let me help you! I saw some astringent here someplace…"

He laughed and backed away, holding up his hands defensively. Half of his jaw was clean shaven, the other half still covered with white foam streaked with a dash of red. "It's nothing. Happens all the time."

"It does?" Not to any man she knew. Her grandfather, for example, had a barber who came by daily to perform that chore.

Zane stepped back up to the mirror. "It's easy to see you never had any brothers." He finished quickly, splashed away the traces of shaving cream with running water, winked at her and walked out of the room.

Jake and Kathy dropped by often to offer help and support of many kinds: a freshly baked cake, a batch of new magazines, a telephone message given or received. They were always welcome, and for a time, Dara would try to lose herself in their comfortable world.

But always, there was Zane…and there was nothing comfortable about their relationship at all. Instead of becoming easier with each other, they seemed to become ever more tense. Zane…sitting across from her at the table, brushing against her as he passed her in a doorway, looking at her with narrow, watchful eyes when she stumbled out of the bedroom in the mornings wearing nothing but one of his flannel shirts for a nightgown.

She had no idea how this enforced intimacy was affecting him, but it was getting to her in major ways. By the time Christmas Day rolled around, she felt drawn tight as a drum. Dressed in her new jeans and boots and her old white silk shirt, she joined him in the living room, where he was folding up his bedding.

He looked her over with obvious approval. "You ready to go on over to headquarters?"

By now she knew that "headquarters" was the main family ranch compound, where the other Farleys lived. She'd never been there but was looking forward to it.

The ride overflowed with beauty. Dreamily, she remembered visions of white Christmases imagined but never realized. Snow frosted the evergreen limbs and fences, lending a smoothness to fields and pastures. The countryside looked like a greeting card, it was so perfect.

They passed beneath a huge arched gate over a cattle guard. She'd learned what those grates placed between the gateposts to keep stock from straying were called now, she realized proudly. A sign hung over the road: Bar F Ranch, The Farley Brothers.

They drove into the ranch yard. Dara glanced around, impressed. Everything looked so neat and spruced up, from the sturdy whitewashed fences with their topping of snow to the welcoming covered porch fronting the sprawling two-story ranch house. A wreath that looked homemade adorned the front door, its big red bow and streamers fluttering cheerfully in a chilly wind.

Zane killed the engine and gave her an oblique glance. "Ready?" he challenged.

She swallowed hard. "Ready!"

Together they loaded up the packages and went inside to enjoy the kind of holiday celebration Dara had never even imagined.

Farley holiday meals always featured turkey, since beef was the staple of everyday life. Over the years when their father, Jim, had been doing the cooking, the turkey tended to be as dry and chewy as pemmican, with stuffing that tasted like cardboard. Since Kathy had joined the family, however, the turkey had been brought to the table brown and succulent and filled with mouthwatering apple-sausage stuffing.

Kathy was a wonderful cook, but Zane didn't think Jake had known when he married her what a prize he was getting—didn't care, in fact. The two had been so crazy in love that nothing else mattered.

Not like Zane and Dara at all.

With another of Kathy's wonderful holiday dinners consumed, Zane watched his new wife help clear the table, scurrying between kitchen and dining room with hands full of dishes. He couldn't help smiling. One thing about Dara, she tried hard; she'd been in the kitchen ever since they arrived. But for how long? When would this cease to be "fun" and start to be work?

Kathy stuck her head through the open doorway. "Everybody ready for dessert?"

"Hooray!" Missy shouted.

"Hooray!" joined in Shane and his father. Jake was acting just like a big kid himself.

"All right, then. But first—Zane, get ready for a surprise!" She turned with a flourish to present...

Dara, walking as carefully as if she were on a tightrope, her full attention centered on the pie she gripped firmly in hands held chest high. She carried it straight to Zane and placed it on the table before him.

Only then did she look at him, her cheeks flushed and her eyes sparkling. "Merry Christmas," she said softly. "I didn't have any money—" she glanced ruefully around the table "—as everybody is well aware.

I don't know how to sew or make things—crafts or stuff like that. So I baked you an apple pie, Zane, my very first. Kathy's even got ice cream to go with it.''

''You baked this pie?'' Zane stared down at it, stunned, and then into his wife's face.

She nodded proudly. ''But in all fairness, Kathy—''

''I never laid a finger on that pie!'' Kathy shouted from the doorway. ''I may have bossed a little and I did give her my recipe, but Dara did it all herself. She'll be able to bake a pie any time she wants after this, she's that quick a learner. Now, for the rest of you guys…'' She walked into the room carrying a pie plate on each palm. The Farleys were not ''cake'' people. ''I've got one pumpkin and one coconut cream, so what'll it be?''

Jake cupped his hands around his mouth, a devilish gleam in his eyes. ''But I want apple!'' he yelled.

Zane joined in the general laughter before telling his brother, ''That may be what you want, but you're not getting any of *this* pie. Didn't you hear what my wife said? She baked this special just for me. It's my Christmas present and I'm going to eat every crumb.'' He picked up his fork, grinned at Dara and dug in without even waiting for the ice cream.

Dara's heart, already soft where he was concerned, turned to mush.

Night fell quickly in Colorado in December. With the gifts opened and dinner dishes washed and put away, Dara and Zane prepared to leave.

Missy gave Dara a hug. "I love my book, Aunt Dara. Thank you so much!"

Dara smiled. "And thank you for the place mats you made and decorated all by yourself. I'm very impressed. I'll treasure them always."

Missy laughed incredulously. "But they're made of paper! I don't think they'll *last* forever."

"Then I'll frame them and put them on the wall," Dara promised. She turned toward her husband. "I'm ready, Zane, if—"

"Aha!" Jake pointed to the ceiling. He'd enjoyed the holiday more than anyone, judging by almost constant smiles. "Not so fast, girl. Zane, your pretty little wife is standing smack-dab under the mistletoe." The mistletoe was held over her head by Jake himself, grinning impishly. "Give her a good one, little brother," he teased. "After that pie, you owe her *something*."

Dara supposed that was an oblique reference to the fact that Zane hadn't given her a gift. But he'd already done so much for her that she really hadn't expected—

Zane stepped close to her and coherent thought ceased abruptly.

"Can't mess with tradition," he said in that slow drawl. Putting his hands on her shoulders, he lifted her to meet his kiss.

Dara closed her eyes, her lips softening at the first light touch of his. Tentative in the beginning, the kiss grew instantly possessive, as if he'd been keeping all kinds of strong emotions bottled up inside. Drawing her against his chest, he pressed her there with one hand on the small of her back.

Too soon, he lifted his head. "Merry Christmas," he said with a smile that looked strained at this close range.

"Hoo-eee!" Jake chortled with delight. "That's putting mistletoe to its proper use, cowboy!"

Dara had actually forgotten they weren't alone, so lost had she been in Zane's embrace. Now she looked around the room at all the approving smiles and felt her cheeks burn with mortification.

If they only knew...

"Have a good time?"

Leaning back dreamily against the pickup seat, Dara rolled her head toward Zane. Seen in profile as he drove, he looked strong and in control of his world.

"Wonderful," she murmured. "I never imagined that kind of family celebration."

"You had a family," he said, curiosity tingeing his tone.

"Yes. When my parents were still alive and to-gether..." She sighed. "They were never home for the holidays. Blythe and I were always shipped off to Grandfather's."

He frowned. "What kind of parents wouldn't spend the holidays with their kids?"

"The kind who'd rather go to Cannes or Monaco or just about anyplace else."

"Your grandfather...?"

"Did his best, I'm sure. But everything was so for-mal. We'd dress in our Sunday best on Christmas

morning before coming downstairs. Following breakfast, we'd be led into the solarium where the tree had
been set up and professionally decorated—we were
never allowed to lay a hand on that tree. Then we'd
sit quietly while one of the servants handed out the
gifts.''

''That,'' Zane said emphatically, ''is downright
pitiful.''

Dara had to laugh. ''In retrospect, I agree. At the
time, I naturally thought that was the way everybody
did it. Eventually, I realized how wrong I was, but
this is the first time I've been part of a real family
holiday.''

Zane stopped the pickup before the cabin door and
turned off the engine. Shifting around to face her in
the dark cab of the truck, he reached out to cover her
hand, which lay on her knee. ''You've got a real family now. I hope we didn't overwhelm you with our
crazy ways.''

She swallowed hard. ''Not at all. Everyone was
wonderful.'' For a moment, she chewed on her lower
lip, trying to decide how much more she should say.
''Especially…you, Zane.''

His hand tightened convulsively on hers, and without another word, he threw open his door and slid
out, pulling her behind him. On the ground, he lifted
her off the seat and into his arms. Turning, he held
her tight against his chest while he carried her up the
steps and into the house.

Standing her on her feet, he flicked on the overhead
light. In the sudden brilliance, his face seemed un-

expectedly strained. She stared at him in astonishment. What in the world had she done?

"Wonderful?" he said, his voice taut. "I'm not sure how wonderful I can risk being. But I can tell you one thing for sure." He pulled her into his arms. "It's getting easier and easier to be wonderful to you, and harder and harder to keep my head when I'm around you...."

He kissed her then with a hungry passion that took her breath away. Dimly, she realized how much he must have been holding back when Jake instigated the kiss beneath the mistletoe complete with audience. This time, there was no such restraint on Zane's part.

Or on her part, either. She'd waited so long to know the fire of him that now she gladly slipped her arms around his neck and rose to meet him. What a relief to know her desire for him was returned. What a relief—

He thrust her away from him and stepped back, breathing hard. Something wild glowed in his dark eyes. "This is no good," he growled. "I'm not ready to make this kind of commitment."

"But..." She pushed tousled hair away from her face with hands that trembled. "We're married! I don't understand."

"Being married should mean more than a license to sleep together." His face was set in tense lines of strain. "There should be an emotional commitment and I'm not ready to make that yet. I don't think you are, either."

His words were slings and arrows to her hopes and dreams. Not for all the world would she open herself further to his disdain. "Whatever you say." She lifted her chin, clamping her teeth together to stop the trembling.

A crooked little smile lifted one corner of his mouth. "I figured you'd understand." He dug around in the pocket of his heavy jacket, pulling out a small, unwrapped jeweler's box. "I did get you a present, by the way."

"You did?" She stared at him, completely confused. Why hadn't he given it to her before? Why choose to give it to her now, when she felt completely demoralized?

"It's something you should have had a long time ago," he muttered, fumbling at the box. "I was remiss. I apologize for the oversight."

"What in the world are you talking about?" She watched him finally pry open the lid, mystified by his suddenly uneasy manner. Leaning forward, she looked into the box he still held without offering it to her.

On a bed of white velvet lay two perfect golden circles, one large and one small but both perfectly plain.

Wedding rings.

Quick tears of surprise and pleasure sprang to her eyes and she was unable to say a single word. All she could do was stare at him and then at the rings, her lips parted and her breathing quick and uneven.

He grabbed her left hand and thrust the smaller of the rings on her third finger. He slipped the other on his own hand.

"People have been talking," he said as if that explained everything. "They don't mind being surprised, but our getting married was more in the nature of *shock*. Until we know what the hell we're doing... Well, maybe this will show them that our marriage is not a joke, and at the same time, protect you from gossip."

The word "protect" brought with it a wave of warm feeling. How like him to want to protect her, even though she couldn't possibly have cared less about what people might say or think. All she cared about was him and whether or not their make-believe marriage was going to become the real thing or go the way of other impossible dreams.

She touched the shiny new ring with the fingers of her right hand. She *was* a married woman. Really.

And her husband was heading back out the front door. "Where are you going?" she cried in alarm.

He paused just long enough to say, "Got a few chores to take care of. Don't wait up."

She was alone. She was devastated.

She was mystified. What was going on here? Why was he so determined to keep their relationship platonic?

It was almost as if...as if his heart was otherwise engaged.

The new year arrived, and with it, more snow and cold weather. But Dara was discovering a strange and wonderful thing about Colorado; the temperature might be twenty degrees, but in all likelihood, the sun would still shine in a blue sky. This happy state of affairs worked miracles with her mental outlook.

Both she and Zane were working hard, he mostly outdoors with the horses and cattle, and she inside, where her efforts were beginning to pay off in a clean and cheery atmosphere. Slim returned from Taos and moved into the bunkhouse right on schedule and she greeted him like a long-lost friend.

She prepared a special dinner the day Slim arrived, spending hours in the kitchen and humming happily to herself while she worked. She was sure that having him around would put Zane more at ease. Sometimes she'd find her husband looking at her with an unreadable expression, which might be skepticism, might be something else.

But on that particular night, he was as happy with their guest as she was. When she dished up the chicken-fried steak and mashed potatoes, everyone dived in with enthusiasm.

"Mmm..." Slim savored his meal. "Good vittles, Dary."

"Glad you like it," she responded with a smile. "If you didn't like my cooking, you could starve to death around here."

Slim forked up another piece of steak. "Now, Dary, you don't thank this old bachelor is movin' in on you lovebirds, do you?"

"Why, I..." She glanced at Zane for guidance.

"Never happen," Slim said emphatically. "There's a little kitchen in the bunkhouse and I know how to use it."

He meant what he said, so she didn't see as much of him as she'd have liked. He pitched in with enthusiasm to help Zane with the ranch chores but remained adamant in his insistence that the honeymooners needed their space.

She'd have been delighted to spend her time with Zane, but he was so rarely around that she took refuge in her pride in what she'd done and continued to do. The house was shaping up nicely, she thought now, surveying the living room with hands on hips. It had taken a lot of elbow grease and a ton of soapsuds, but everything was now clean and shiny. Beneath the dirt and grime and layers of trash, the furniture was actually wonderful, most of it handmade from native woods, roughly hewn but lovingly conceived.

The Farleys were pioneers in these parts, she'd learned from idle comments of Zane and Kathy and Jake but most of all from Slim. Well-known and respected, they were a force to be reckoned with in these Rocky Mountains.

But every night when the day's work was done, Slim retired to the bunkhouse, and if she was lucky, it was just the two of them again: Zane and Dara, Dara and Zane. The long, quiet evenings were her favorite time of day. Sitting together before a blazing fireplace, they'd read or work on small portable chores. He'd mend bridles and polish tack, while she'd try to sew on buttons and mend rips and tears in his jeans and shirts.

She was getting better at that, too, she thought proudly. Jabbing her needle back into the bright red tomato-shaped pincushion, she stifled a sigh.

The more time she spent with Zane Farley, the more convinced she became that…that what she felt for him went far beyond…

He looked up suddenly and caught her watching him. She smiled. He didn't. Seated before the fire with leather scraps and straps strewn around him, he shifted restlessly.

"Can you hand me that awl?" He pointed.

She picked up the sharp instrument he indicated, but instead of merely handing it to him, she knelt before him and offered it, handle first. "Zane...?"

"What is it?"

She licked her lips. "I wonder..." No sound intruded beyond the snap and crackle of the fire behind him. Its warmth felt good on her arms. His hands would have felt better. "Would you teach me to ride?"

"Ride horses?" He looked astonished.

She smiled. "What else? If I could ride, maybe I could—you know, help you out sometimes. Spend more time with you..."

"Don't you have enough to do around here without taking on more?"

"I keep pretty busy, but mostly that's because I don't know what I'm doing half the time," she said, opting yet again for honesty. "As I get better, it takes less time."

His expression softened. "You *are* getting better. I wouldn't want you to think I haven't noticed."

She flushed with pleasure. "Thank you. That's nice to hear."

"But about learning to ride, do you think you'll be here—" He bit off his words but not in time. He'd been about to say, "Do you think you'll be here *long enough to bother?*" or something to that effect.

"My God," she whispered, staring at him with wide eyes, "you don't have any faith in me at all, do you?"

He stood up, his face hard again. "Sorry. I didn't mean to insult you. As it happens, I won't be able to teach you, at least not right away."

She rose to stand before him. "Got a big project coming up? That's okay. I can wait."

"Not a big project." His dark eyes narrowed. "Maybe you should have Slim teach you. I could speak to him if you like."

Suddenly out of patience, she astonished herself by stamping a foot. "I don't want Slim to do it! If I did, I'd ask him myself."

"Suit yourself." He moved toward the door as if eager to escape her.

"Why?"

"Why what?"

"Why won't you teach me if you don't have some big project coming up?"

"Because," he said, not meeting her eyes, "I won't be here. I'm heading out day after tomorrow to hit a couple of rodeos before I get so far behind the curve that I'll never catch up again."

And he walked out of the house, closing the door firmly between himself and the book she sent hurtling after him.

CHAPTER TEN

LUNCH was ready, but Zane wasn't there to eat it. Annoyed, nerves stretched taut by the tense atmosphere left in the wake of his announcement of the day before, Dara threw on her jacket and stomped out toward the barn. He might be off somewhere on horseback or in the pickup, but if he was within walking distance, she was prepared to give him a piece of her mind for failing to appear at the usual time.

Stepping from a world of sunlight glittering off ice and snow into the pleasant twilight of the barn, she closed the big door behind her and looked around.

He was nowhere to be seen.

"Zane?" She took a hesitant step forward. Several stanchions for cattle were on the left-hand side of the double doors, stalls for horses on the right. All were empty. She'd only been in here a few times, not feeling particularly welcome in his domain. "Lunch!" she called out, her voice echoing in the stillness. "Zane, are you here?"

No answer. She hesitated, wondering where he'd gone. At that moment, several sprigs of hay drifted down from the loft above.

Dara looked up, expecting to see him peering down at her. He wasn't. Planting her hands on her hips, she glared at the large square opening offering ladder access to the loft. "Zane Farley, you answer me!" she demanded indignantly.

When he didn't, she stepped up to the wooden ladder and put her hands on a rung. If he wouldn't come down to her, she'd go up to him! She began to climb hand over hand. Poking her head through the opening, she scanned the area revealed to her. She saw nothing but stacks of hay, some bales broken open as if he'd been forking the fodder down to the animals below.

Zane himself wasn't there. Where could he have—

"Dara! What the hell are you doing up there?"

His loud voice coming from below her was so unexpected that she started, the sole of one shoe slipping on the wooden rung. With a little shriek of alarm, she grabbed for a better handhold. Hay rolled beneath her scrabbling fingers and she felt her body pitch backward off the ladder and into space.

Zane caught her in his arms, but the momentum of her fall carried them both over backward into a pile of hay he'd tossed down earlier in the day. She landed on top of him, knocking the breath from his body. For a moment, he just lay there gasping and holding her safe in his arms.

She groaned.

He fought for enough oxygen to speak. "Are you okay? Dammit, Dara, if you've gone and gotten yourself hurt, I'll—"

"You'll *what?*" She struggled to break his hold but without success.

Yeah, what? he asked himself. If she'd been hurt—which he now doubted—it would be his fault and he'd never forgive himself. But he wasn't going to tell *her* that.

His breathing was returning to normal at last. "Never mind that. Tell me you're okay."

"I'm okay."

"Say it like you mean it, dammit!"

"I'm okay, Zane." She resumed the struggle. "Turn me loose!"

"Not until you tell me what the hell you were doing climbing that ladder with those stupid shoes."

"Don't you call my shoes stupid!" She managed to hoist herself up on her elbows so she could glare down into his face. Blond hair tumbled fetchingly around her flushed cheeks and her green eyes flashed fire.

"They're stupid to climb ladders with." It was difficult to concentrate on speech when she was so enticingly close to him. "The soles are slick and the shoes are flimsy." With their heavy jackets between them, all he felt from the waist up was a fluffy bundle. From the waist down, with only two layers of denim between them, all he felt was the heat of her burning into him like a torch.

"I wouldn't have climbed the ladder if you'd answered me when I called," she objected.

"I was out back, I guess." He shifted, and that minute movement allowed her lower body to settle more snugly against his. He saw her eyes fly open in reaction and she stiffened. But she stopped trying to pull away from him.

She licked those luscious lips. "It's...lunchtime,"

she said, her formerly indignant voice dropping to a sexy pitch.

"Is it?" All he wanted to do was lie there and hold her…at least for starters. He twisted the fingers of one hand through the silky blond curls framing her face.

"Aren't you hungry?" she whispered, letting the persistent pressure of his hand guide her face nearer to his.

He wanted to groan; he wanted to tell her he was hungry all right—for her. But he didn't want to give her that kind of power over him, so he said instead, "I've got to finish up out back first. Then…I'll be in."

"No hurry." Her lips nearly touched his when she spoke. "Zane, do you suppose…do you think maybe…oh, Zane…"

"Do I suppose what?" The warmth and softness of her breath was like nectar.

She let her mouth brush across his. "That you might change your mind about going and—"

He flipped her over so suddenly that she shrieked. Before she could pull herself together, he was on his feet and towering over her.

Leaning to one side, she rubbed her derriere gingerly. "What was that for?" she asked plaintively.

"For trying to use sex to get your own way," he flung at her.

"Use…?" She stared up at him, her eyes quickly going dark and turbulent. "How dare you! Zane Farley, you are the most conceited, arrogant, stubborn…"

He knew all that and he wasn't going to wait to hear her tell him what he already knew.

Use sex to get her own way? She was so incensed at the suggestion that for the next two days, she barely spoke to him except to answer direct questions. If he even noticed her attempts to give him the silent treatment, he didn't let on as he went about business as usual. When the time came for him to hitch up the horse trailer and load Scout, she considered locking herself in the bathroom until he'd gone—but finally decided not to.

What would that gain? she wondered. Bundled in her heavy jacket, she stood beside the rig near the snowy corral and watched him work. The way he kept glancing her way, you'd almost think—

A sudden thought crashed in on her. *You'd think he expected her to disappear in a puff of smoke at any minute.*

You'd think he didn't really expect her to be here when he came back.

Well, maybe she wouldn't be! As things stood now, she wasn't his wife at all. She was a maid and cook and all-around servant. The things a wife would do for love were demeaning without it—and at this point, she was no longer sure she would ever win his respect, let alone his love.

He approached, his eyes shimmering in brilliant sunlight that made her squint even behind her dark glasses. He looked very tall and handsome, standing there before the backdrop of snowcapped mountains. His warm breath created a vapor cloud before him.

"I'm heading out now," he said in a flat, cool voice.

For a moment, she just stared at him. Then she said, "Will you be coming back?"

He frowned as if he didn't understand the question. "This is my home. Of course I'll be coming back."

"Care to tell me when?" She could be cool, too.

He sighed. "Now, Dara, don't be that way."

"What way?"

"The way you've been ever since I told you I was leaving. Hell, you knew my line of work when you married me." He looked offended in the extreme.

She was offended, too. "I don't object to your going so much as I object to not being consulted," she flared. "You wouldn't treat me this way if I was really your wife."

"You *are* my wife." His mouth tightened as if he knew that to his regret. "What do you think that ring on your left hand means?"

"It takes more than a ring and more than a piece of paper. It takes a commitment I'm not sure I'm ever going to get out of you."

"Look who's talking," he said softly, his dark gaze boring into her. "I told you I'd be back, but you haven't told me you'll be here when I do."

Their stormy glances met, his forming a question. No, she thought, you're not going to get around me that easily. Not this time!

Rising on tiptoe, she planted a quick, hard kiss square on his lips, then stepped away before he could grab her.

Which he tried to do. When his arms came up

empty, he flexed his fingers, and his eyes glittered with anger. "What was that for?"

"For the road," she said airily, trying to goad him into reacting. "Don't I have a right to kiss my own husband without being accused of having ulterior motives?"

"About that..." He looked distinctly uncomfortable. "I'm sorry I—"

"Don't give it a thought," she interrupted. "Have a good time and win lots of money."

"You still haven't answered my original question," he called after her, his tone strident. "Will *you* be here when I get back? Because I'll never chase after you—"

"Gee, if you don't know the answer to that, I guess you'll just have to wait and find out."

That was such a lie that she ran inside and slammed the door, afraid he'd come after her and demand the truth. But he didn't. To her dismay, he merely stood there for another minute, head cocked and eyes narrowed thoughtfully. Then he climbed into the pickup and drove away.

When the pickup and horse trailer were out of sight, she ran outside and jumped into the little Jeep he'd borrowed for her from the Farley fleet of vehicles. Grinding gears, she took off for headquarters and a sympathetic ear. At this point, it seemed as if Kathy Farley was the only woman on earth who might possibly understand the Farley men.

Kathy poured coffee into heavy mugs and carried them to the table before the big kitchen window. Dara accepted hers with a grateful sigh.

Kathy frowned. "My goodness, what are you so down about? We all expected him to hit the rodeo circuit long before now, honey. Don't worry. He'll be back."

"Will he?" Too depressed to put a good face on it, Dara poured cream into her cup and added a heaping spoonful of sugar.

"You know he will." Kathy looked thoughtful. "Dara, I get the feeling that you're having a hard time figuring out how Zane's mind works."

Dara had to laugh, although ruefully. "Most of the time, I don't have a *clue!*"

"In that case, I think it's time I told you a few things about the Farley boys."

Dara sighed. "I wish *somebody* would. Zane certainly doesn't talk about himself."

Kathy nodded agreement. "He never has." She fidgeted for a moment. "Did you know their mother walked out on them and their father?" she asked at last.

"I kind of suspected something like that," Dara admitted, "although no one has ever told me in so many words."

Kathy stared at her cup. "She just up and left. It almost killed their father, and of course, it affected both boys...but especially Zane. He'd been her favorite and thought it was his fault, according to Jake. Zane was only five or six, Dara. I'm not sure he's ever really trusted a female since."

"How could she do it?" Dara wondered. How could *any* woman leave her husband and children?

Kathy sighed. "We'll never know. She's dead now. But what she did made all the Farley men woman shy, to some extent or other. When I fell for Jake—" she rolled her eyes "—he was impossible. If I'd waited for him to make a move, I'd be a spinster today."

Dara had to smile at that, having seen them together and well aware that Jake adored his wife. "You mean *you* went after *him?*"

"With a vengeance!" Kathy looked extremely proud of herself. "I got him, too. And you've got Zane, complete with wedding ring. He'll loosen up just like his brother did, but you'll have to give him time. He has to learn to trust all over again." She winked one conspiratorial eye. "You'll tame him, honey. I have complete confidence in you."

Dara wasn't quite so sure. "Do you think so?"

"I know so."

"It's a little tough when he's off at some rodeo somewhere."

"But he'll be back." Kathy smiled. "When he walks in, you'll be ready for him." Her smile grew wider. "A guy is a guy is a guy. Subtlety is not prized by guys, if you catch my drift."

Dara sat up straighter. She *would* be ready—and she wouldn't be subtle. If Zane thought that little tussle in the barn was an attempt to seduce him, he was in for a revelation. Zane Farley wouldn't know what hit him.

The two women spoke of other things then, shared laughter and family gossip, enjoyed lunch with the children and together put Shane down for his nap. Dara held his sweet, warm little body in her arms and breathed deeply of his baby scent.

Kathy watched with a smile. "You're good with him," she said approvingly. "I can tell you like children because they like you, too. Kids know who they can trust."

Dara tucked the satin binding of the baby blanket beneath the pudgy chin and dropped one final kiss on Shane's button nose. "I have a niece I'm very fond of."

"You and Zane will make wonderful parents someday," Kathy predicted cheerfully, as if it was a done deal. Leading the way from the bedroom, she elaborated, "He's always adored Missy and Shane and they're crazy about him, too."

Children, Zane's children. Dara had never even allowed herself to dream that impossible dream. "Maybe someday," she said, deliberately vague. "Thanks for everything, Kathy, but I think it's time I headed back—"

The telephone rang. With a hand, Kathy gestured for Dara to wait just a minute and went to answer. Dara picked up a magazine and sat down to wait to finish her goodbyes, thinking about how lonely the cabin was going to be without Zane.

"Dara. *Dara!*"

She started. "I'm sorry. What is it?"

Kathy held out the receiver. "It's for you," she whispered. "Your grandfather!"

Dara responded with reluctance. If Donald Linnell noticed any lack of enthusiasm, he didn't let on.

"How are you, Princess?" he asked.

"I'm fine. How are you and Blythe and Jenny?"

"Fine, just fine. Are you happy?"

Was she happy? Who knew! "Of course I'm happy," she told him firmly.

"You don't sound all that happy to me. As a matter of fact, I thought you might be a little down with your husband away."

"How do you know he's not here?" she demanded.

"I have my sources," he said smoothly.

"Then your sources also must have told you he's just going to a couple of rodeos and will be back within a week."

"But in the meantime you're all alone in the middle of nowhere," he baited her. "Princess, why don't you come home? Even if it's just for a visit. We'd all love to see you. I can arrange to have a ticket waiting for you at Denver International Airport whenever you say."

"No, no, I couldn't." But it was tempting. She hadn't realized how much she'd miss her sister and her niece. In some ways, she even missed her grandfather, if not his meddling ways.

"Why not?" he wheedled. "You can return any time you want...*if* you want. We could throw a party, invite your friends—"

"My friends are in Colorado now," she interrupted fiercely. "Thanks, but no thanks. I'm staying right here." She cast a determined glance at Kathy. "I'm not going to take a chance on being away when my husband returns. As a matter of fact, I...I'm planning a big homecoming for him for—" she was struck by sudden inspiration "—for Valentine's Day. He wouldn't want to miss that." She crossed her fingers.

Kathy flashed a thumb's-up and a big grin.

"So tell everyone I said hello and that I'm fine and loving my new life," Dara concluded.

"But, Dara—"

"*Please* stop trying to cause trouble, Grandfather," she pleaded. "I don't want your money and I don't want your interference."

"Then what *do* you want from me, Princess?" He sounded frustrated, as if he couldn't figure out her true meaning.

"Just your love," she said. "Just your love."

She hung up the phone, blinking back tears.

It wasn't that Zane exactly succeeded in putting her out of his mind, but he did manage to turn all that pent-up emotion into a couple of winning rodeos. He took the calf roping two out of two and the steer wrestling once, with a close second in the other.

He still had it, he thought with satisfaction. Heading the pickup down the road toward home, he admitted to himself that he'd been right to take a few weeks off after the National Finals and let his body heal from the rigors of the past rodeo season before starting on the new one.

He'd been so banged up that Las Vegas had been hell; otherwise he wouldn't have taken that painkiller from Shorty, which also meant he wouldn't be a married man today.

Or would he?

Maybe Slim was right about fate. Maybe everything would have ended up the same way, simply reached by a different path. Pulling into the yard before the cabin, he killed the engine.

And realized his heart was banging away against his ribs a mile a minute. Would she be here or would she already have given up and returned to her grandfather and a life of glittering captivity? He now believed that giving her a wedding ring for Christmas had been the height of stupidity. He banged one leather-gloved palm on the steering wheel in frustration. That ring would be just one more thing for her to leave behind when she left.

And then he'd gone and compounded his error on this trip by bringing back something else for her, something that was bound to bring him more grief. She'd been furious with him when he left, but he'd told himself that wasn't why he'd brought her a present.

Was he kidding himself? Was he just trying to jolly her out of a bad mood, assuming she was still here to *be* jollied?

Regardless, he'd be damned if he'd sit here in the snowy front yard any longer and worry about it. He'd know soon enough, but first he had to take care of Scout…and Dara's four-legged present, a beautiful little pinto mare.

Old Scout had never let him down. Zane wouldn't let the sorrel horse down, either—or anyone or anything else that deserved his loyalty. Regardless of his burning desire to know what he'd find inside the cabin, he set about methodically unloading the animals, checking them over, brushing them down, watering them and turning them out into the corral with some good Bar F hay to munch on.

Only then did he yank up his collar, tamp down his hat firmly, take a deep breath and turn toward the house. He crossed the yard with determined steps, trying not to anticipate the worst. Without giving himself time to think further about it, he stamped up the steps, threw open the door, stepped inside and bellowed at the top of his lungs, "Dara! I'm home!"

And then he stopped dead in his tracks. Garlands of homemade red paper hearts decorated the room— masses of red paper hearts. What the…? But before he could figure that out, he was distracted by the wonderful aromas assailing his nostrils: baking bread, roasting meat, sizzling apples and cinnamon, perking coffee. And something else…something slightly sweet but still pungent, an aroma almost…flowery.

Something like a woman's perfume…

"Dara," he called again, but this time his voice came out more like a croak and he cleared his throat, suddenly self-conscious. He didn't know what he expected to find here—maybe nothing—but certainly not this.

"I'm here."

At the soft utterance, he spun around. He'd been staring at the kitchen, but her voice had come from the other direction, from the bedroom.

She stood there in the open doorway, wearing those stretchy tight pants women liked so much and a short, little old T-shirt that barely covered her beautiful breasts. Under that, she wasn't wearing a stitch or he was no judge of women. Her feet were bare, her hair tumbling from a cluster on top of her head into a waterfall of curly tendrils. Color flushed her cheeks as if she'd been slaving over a hot stove all day long...or had some other cause for excitement.

"You're home," she said with a satisfaction that came through loud and clear.

"Jake didn't tell you I was comin'?" Zane tossed his hat on the rack and shrugged out of his heavy jacket.

"I haven't seen Jake lately, but since this is Valentine's Day..." She gave him a melting smile. "Welcome home, Zane. It's been lonesome around here."

"Yeah, well..." He shifted from one booted foot to the other. Jeez, Valentine's Day? "I brought you a present." *Thank God.*

"You mean besides you?"

Startled, he nodded. "Uh..." Eager to change the subject, he sniffed the air with theatrical gestures. "Something sure smells good."

Her smile grew wider. "I've been taking cooking lessons from Kathy while you were gone. I needed something to fill my time."

He swallowed hard, then cleared his throat. "Maybe I should go away more often."

Her eyes narrowed, flashed dangerously. "Just try it, cowboy."

And while he stood there like a statue, staring at her in disbelief, she crossed the space between them, threw her arms around his neck, yanked his head down and pressed her lips to his.

CHAPTER ELEVEN

FOR a moment, she thought she'd made a horrible, horrible mistake. But then his lips warmed and softened against hers, and with a groan, he framed her face with his hands and tilted her head for his kiss.

Deliberately, she pressed her body against his, telling him without words how much she wanted him. She thought he understood when, without even breaking the kiss, he scooped her up into his arms and strode with her across the living room and through the open door of the bedroom.

Sitting on the edge of the bed, he held her across his lap to trail kisses across her closed eyes, her cheeks. At the same time, he stroked her bare midriff, easing one hand up beneath the silly little T-shirt.

He nuzzled her ear. "Your nice dinner…"

"It's in the oven." Her voice came out low and breathy. "Everything will be f-fine.…"

"You're sure of that?" He nibbled on her ear. "After all your work, the cooking lessons and everything, I wouldn't want it to go to waste."

"The only lessons I'm interested in at the moment have nothing to do with food." She arched beneath the pressure of his hands and lips. "Zane, I've missed you so much. You don't know.…"

"Your welcome has given me a fair idea." He twisted his hands through her hair. He was breathing hard and there was a hot, wild light in his dark eyes. "Dara, are you sure this is what you want?"

She stared up at him, her own eyes half-closed. "Don't you?" she challenged.

He smiled tightly, curving lines bracketing his lean cheeks. "Sweetheart, if you have to ask me that, you *do* need lessons."

And rolling over onto his back on the big bed, he proceeded to give her the first one…and shortly after that, the second.

They lay on the tangled bed, reveling in sweet exhaustion. Shadows crept through frosty windows, spreading a muted golden light across Mr. and Mrs. Zane Farley, truly man and wife at last.

Dara was so happy she was afraid she'd start crying if she tried to express her feelings. How she loved this man! Everything she'd gone through since she'd met him—feelings of doubt and rejection and incompetence, every bit of it—was worth this final feeling of complete togetherness.

She would tell him that she loved him.

Her heart stopped beating at the thought. There had never been words of love between them; only words of…*negotiation* sprang to mind. Their marriage had been negotiated: Zane would stand by her against her grandfather and she would be the very best wife she could be. But from the very beginning, she'd felt there could be more to their marriage than that and she'd been right.

Lying nestled against his side with her cheek

pressed to his chest, she shifted enough to allow herself to look up into his face.

He was frowning.

Why was he frowning? Did he regret what had just happened between them? Dara chewed on the inside of her cheek. She didn't dare tell him the depth of her feelings toward him until she was sure such a revelation wouldn't push him farther away.

She kissed his chest almost shyly, which was funny when she considered all that had just passed between them. "Happy Valentine's Day," she murmured. "Zane darling, there's something we need to talk a—"

"Zane! Are you in there, boy?"

Slim, roaring from the front porch. A heavy pounding began on the door.

Zane started as if hit by a bolt of electricity. In the twinkling of an eye, he sprang from the bed and grabbed for his clothing, strewn about the room in haste.

Dara sat up, incredulous, clutching the sheet around her breasts. "Zane, don't go! Slim can wait. We really need to talk about—"

"What? Seems to me there's nothing left to be said." Busy stuffing his shirt into the waistband of his Wranglers, he didn't look at her.

Her heart clenched into a knot of heavy dread. "You're wrong." Her voice trembled and she tried to steady it. "There's everything to be said. We *have* to talk."

He shoved his sockless feet into boots. "Why do

women always have to talk everything to death? I thought it was pretty self-explanatory.''

''Zane! We got us a crisis out here! Scout—''

"Scout!" An expression of absolute horror crossed Zane's face and he bounded for the bedroom door. "If anything happens to that horse—''

"You love that horse more than…!" Dara couldn't go on. What point was there in saying *more than you love me* when he didn't love her at all or even care to hear her profess her love for him?

Besides, she was speaking to an empty space. The front door slammed and she heard pounding footsteps on the porch, then silence. Whatever Slim's emergency was, it meant more to Zane than anything his wife might have to say.

Trembling, dejected, Dara crawled out of bed and dressed. She felt drained, defeated. So much for her grand plan. She was right back where she started, except now she was in love with him. If he never learned to love her back, her heart would be broken; pride was no longer the primary issue.

So why was she still hanging around, waiting for the worst to happen? Without a shred of hope, she wandered into the kitchen, fragrant with the aromas of good food.

But as she bent over the oven to check the roast, the fact that Zane would be back burst upon her. He wasn't gone for good; he was simply going to check his horse. When he'd assured himself that Scout was all right, she'd hear his footsteps on the porch. When she did, she'd be ready for him.

If her physical charms weren't enough to hold him,

she thought wryly, perhaps the meal she'd prepared would do the trick. Anything, just long enough to slow him down so she could tell him…show him… She sucked in a quick, hard breath, knowing that it wasn't going to be easy to convince him that he meant everything to her.

"Easy, boy. Easy there." Zane ran his hands lightly over the trembling legs of the best roping horse west of the Mississippi. The animal rolled his eyes, the whites showing, but held steady.

Slim leaned down to look. "Dagnabbit," he said, "that was too close for comfort. When I found old Scout with both front legs jammed through that rotten wood siding, I thought sure we was lookin' at a disaster. What the hey made him do that, do you suppose?"

"Dunno." Zane lifted one hoof and inspected it with care. "Coulda been a snake or even a rat—hell, a shadow could've done it. Scout gets real high-strung once in a while."

"Wal," Slim said, sounding relieved, "we got off lucky. But when I tried to get him out by my lonesome, he wasn't havin' none of it. That's when I went to get you." He gave the other man an uneasy sideways glance. "I'm sorry about that, Zane. I know you just got home and all, and you and the little lady was prob'ly—"

"Let it go," Zane cut in. He lowered the hoof and straightened, carefully keeping his expression blank. "Scout looks okay, but I think I'd better throw him in the trailer and take him over to Doc Burns just to be sure.''

"I'll do that fer you,'' Slim offered. ''It's the least I can do after—''

"I'll do it myself.'' Realizing how combative he sounded, Zane tried to soften the edge. ''I appreciate the offer, but a man looks after his own horses.''

"That's true.'' Slim glanced toward the house. ''But a man also takes care of his wife, if he's got the sense God give a goose. You seem to be lettin' down in that department, cowboy.''

"Dara been complainin'?'' Zane asked sharply, his head rearing back.

"Hell, no! She never complains about nothin', at least not that I know of. It's just that sometimes I see this…this particular *look* in her eyes, kinda sadlike.''

Zane knew that look and steeled himself against it. ''She knew what I was when she married me.''

"She didn't know *nothin'* when she married you,'' Slim countered. ''Doggone it, boy, why don't you give the girl a chance? She's doin' her best—''

"Can it, Slim, and just tell her where I'm going.''

Grabbing Scout's lead rope, Zane turned his back on the old cowboy and walked away. But he couldn't walk away from what Slim had been trying to tell him.

She's doin' her best…

Slim didn't know the half of it. She'd even gone so far as to seduce her husband, to what end he couldn't imagine. Whatever she wanted from him she could have, everything right up to but not including his love.

When you gave your love, you were vulnerable, without defenses and easily hurt. Zane Farley was not a man who'd let a woman set him up for that kind of fall.

Hell, he thought with grim humor, he was just a cowboy who loved his horse. Scout never let him down. Never looked at another cowboy, never showed the slightest interest in greener pastures. Yep, if he could find a woman as faithful as his horse, he might be willing to take a chance.

But take a chance on that little filly inside the cabin with her sexy body and fetching ways?

He'd sooner be up the same tree with a grizzly.

It jolted Dara, having Slim come hat in hand to tell her that her husband had taken his horse to the doctor.

But that's okay, she tried to soothe herself when she was alone again; he's coming back. And when he does, I'm going to tell him how I feel if I really *do* have to rope and tie him!

So she took down the paper hearts, her own heavy, and did what she could to salvage the meal. Then she sat down to wait.

Hours later when she heard a pickup in the yard, she breathed a sigh of relief but didn't rise from her seat on the sofa. She wouldn't be standing at the door ready to pounce on him this time. She'd let him come in, sit down to a dinner that was well past its prime, then say her piece, which basically went, "I love you! Is there the slightest chance you'll ever love me back? Because if there is, I'm willing to wait forever."

She was, too—if only…if only…

A knock on the door was like a blow to her midsection. Zane wouldn't knock on his own door even if he was angry with her—and why should he be? It wasn't as if she'd greeted him with tears and lamentations.

Crossing the room quickly, she threw open the door to find Slim standing there looking totally miserable. Shifting from booted foot to booted foot, he licked his lips and swallowed hard.

"Why, Slim," she said in surprise, "come on in. What brings you here at this hour?" Which must be nearly nine o'clock, she realized with a start.

"Nah, I better not come in," Slim demurred. Grabbing his hat from his head, he crushed the brim between his fingers. "I gotta…well, I kinda gotta message from yore husband," he stammered.

"Zane?" She glanced past the bowlegged puncher, wondering if Zane was in the barn or—or what? "Where is he? What's going on?"

Slim let out a long, low, mournful groan. "He's gone, is where he is."

"Gone? Gone where?" She was thinking, *I'll kill him if this is true! I'll strangle him with my own hands!*

"Who knows?" Slim asked rhetorically. "Rodeoin', that's all I can say. After Doc give Scout a clean bill a health, Zane just up and decided to light out to the next rodeo. He called headquarters and ast 'em to send somebody to tell you and that fell to me, natur'ly." He looked downright disgusted with that turn of events.

Dara stood there stiff as a poker, repeating to herself over and over again, *I will not cry!* After a moment, she asked, "Did he say when he'd be home?"

Slim shook his head miserably, refusing to meet her gaze.

"I see," she said calmly, but she didn't, not really. "In that case…" She drew a deep breath and squared her shoulders. "In that case, I want you to get yourself in here *immediately.* I cooked for days to get ready for that…!" Calm down, Dara, she ordered herself. "I cooked a special Valentine's Day meal for my husband. It's in that kitchen—" she gestured a bit wildly "—getting all dried out and yucky and *somebody's* going to eat it!"

Slim took a step backward. "Yes, ma'am," he said. "Sure does smell great. I'll make short work of all them vittles. They won't go to waste, I can promise you that."

He hurried inside and she closed the door before following him toward the kitchen.

How could Zane do this to her?

No explanation presented itself. After a few moments, she pulled herself together long enough to put the food on the table. She'd think about it later, she decided. But one thing she wouldn't do was react in kind.

When Zane Farley finally came back home, no matter when it was, he'd find his wife waiting for him.

And waiting for answers.

Time drags when you're miserable, Dara discovered not for the first time. As one day without Zane stretched into another, she found her determination to confront him growing stronger rather than weaker.

If his greatest fear was of abandonment caused by his mother, his wife wasn't going to add to his distrust. He could stay away a year and Dara promised herself she'd still be here waiting.

But oh, how she longed for his return. She almost wished—she *did* wish—she might be pregnant so she'd have someone upon whom to lavish her love. Perhaps then the waiting would be easier. When she realized such was not to be, at least this time, she nearly wept with loneliness and disappointment.

Kathy tried to help but was at a loss to explain her brother-in-law's behavior. When six weeks had passed, she admitted to Dara that the entire family thought Zane had "gone crazy as bedbugs".

Dara just smiled and shrugged. As long as she knew he was true to his marriage vows, as she was to hers, she could get through this. Even a troublemaking telephone call from her grandfather failed to shake her resolve.

Then in early April, on a day filled with sunshine and the warm promise of spring, a strange pickup truck pulled into the yard and stopped. Dara, who'd been hanging sheets on the clothesline, stood there with a mouth full of clothespins, wondering who'd come to visit her.

To her surprise, a woman alighted. Dropping the pins into a container suspended from the clothesline, Dara started forward. Hospitality was a way of life in these mountains. Whoever this might prove to be, she'd be welcome.

Dara shaded her eyes with a hand and smiled. "May I help you?" she asked as the woman drew closer.

The woman smiled back. She was in her late twenties, Dara guessed, and well endowed to boot. Her fire-engine red jeans were skintight, and the matching shirt strained to cover full breasts. Over that, she wore a fringed leather vest sporting fancy beading with matching beading on her white Stetson.

If that wasn't intimidating enough, she was at least four inches taller than Dara and a whole lot brassier, with less-than-subtle makeup and billowing blond hair beneath her hat.

The newcomer stuck out her hand. "Hi. I'm Jody Mitchell."

"Dara Farley." Dara shook hands, still puzzled. "Uh...have we met? In Las Vegas last December, maybe?"

Jody shook her head. "You mean at your wedding?"

"That's right. There were so many of Zane's friends there that I had trouble keeping everyone straight."

Jody laughed. "If I'da been there, you'd have remembered. Actually, I'm a...a friend of Zane's." She hesitated, suddenly looking a trifle less confident. "He's never mentioned me?"

Dara cocked her head, puzzled by the woman's attitude. "Not that I recall."

"I'm a barrel racer."

"Really! How interesting." Dara glanced toward

the house. "Would you like to come in for a cup of coffee? Zane isn't here but—"

"I know he's not," Jody agreed hastily. "I came...well, I guess I came to see you."

"Me?" Taken aback, Dara waited. "Why?"

"To see what kind of woman finally hooked Zane Farley."

"Oh, I didn't hook—"

"Sure you did. And if I'da known what kind of bait was going to work, I'd have put it on my line long ago." Jody sighed. "Sorry about that. It's just that I've known Zane for a long time and kept company with him up until—well, you know."

"I don't know at all." But Dara did know about that shaft of foreboding arcing down her spine.

"He never told you?"

"Told me what?"

"That me and him was—"

The sound of thundering hoofbeats brought her swinging around. Slim galloped into the yard, dismounting before his horse had even come to a full stop. For a man his age, he was remarkably spry.

"Jody!" he exploded. "What the hell are—what are you doing here?"

"Nice to see you, too, Slim."

Slim glanced anxiously at Dara. "You've met Zane's little woman?"

"Sure. I was just telling her—"

"I don't think you've got any business telling her nothin'."

Dara was astonished by his hostility. "Hush, Slim." She touched his sleeve lightly. "Jody was just about to tell me that she and Zane have been..." She searched for possibilities. "Friends? Neighbors?" And of course, a final possibility occurred to her. "L-lovers?"

"Bingo!" Jody chimed in.

"Jody!" Slim clenched gnarled hands into fists. "Why'd you have to go and say that?"

"Because it's true," the blond cowgirl declared. "I'm not here to cause trouble, but she asked and I can't see lyin' about it."

Dara's mouth felt powder dry. "When did you—I mean, when did you and Zane...break up? You did break up, didn't you?"

"Oh, sure." Jody shrugged. "Actually, now that you mention it, it was the day you two got married. Or should I say the night?"

Slim let out an inarticulate groan. "You shouldn't say nothin'! Whaddaya mean, comin' here and causin' trouble? And all this time I thought you was a nice gal."

Jody rolled her eyes. "Settle down, Slim. I *didn't* come to cause trouble. I came for two completely different reasons. The first one was to see the woman who could do what I couldn't—get Zane Farley to the altar. I tried to do it by telling him I was engaged to somebody else and you see how that worked out."

Dara murmured, "So *that's* what happened. That's why he was in such a funny mood that night."

"Could be," Jody agreed.

Dara licked parched lips. "And the other reason?"

"Yeah, that." Jody shoved her left hand into the slash pocket of her jeans, which wasn't easy considering how tight they were. After considerable scenic movement, she snaked her hand out again. Obviously holding something concealed in her fist, she held it out.

Dara automatically extended her own hand.

"I came to return this," Jody said, and uncoiled her fingers.

A battered golden ring fell onto Dara's palm: Zane's wedding band.

CHAPTER TWELVE

"THAT'S the last straw!"

"Dary, calm yourself," Slim pleaded, following her in her restless circuit of the room. "You don't know how Jody come by Zane's ring."

"And she sure wasn't interested in telling me, was she?" She stopped pacing so suddenly that he ran up her heels. The fleeting pain felt good, diverting her from her rage for at least a few seconds.

Slim caught her by the shoulders to hold her still long enough to listen to him. "Dary, honey, you didn't give her a chance to explain. For a minute there, I thought you wuz gonna jump her good—and so did she. Trust me, she's sorry she ever set foot on the Bar F and she ain't gonna make that mistake again, no sirree-bob." His eyes widened. "Who woulda thought it? You plumb scared her off."

"Good riddance," Dara muttered through gritted teeth. Her nails, no longer perfectly manicured ovals, cut into her palms. "How dare Zane do this to me, his wife? How dare he not tell me about *that woman!*"

"So who you gonna believe, Zane or some pore loser? Don't you think it's possible she wuz keener on him than he wuz on her? Heck, she said flat out she set her traps for him."

"They were lovers," Dara reminded him in a deadly voice.

"Now, we don't know that fer sure," Slim argued. "And even if they wuz, she didn't claim it wuz recent."

"Then how'd she get his ring when he was wearing it when he left? I thought he had a little respect for the institution of...the institution of...m-marriage...." She couldn't go on. What had happened seemed as painfully obvious to her as Slim's loyal determination to defend his friend's honor.

Zane had left angry; why, she still hadn't figured out. At one rodeo or another, he'd run into his old flame, Jody, who'd indicated a willingness to pick up where they left off. They'd renewed old *relationships* and Zane had proven his commitment to Jody by removing his wedding ring, the symbol of his failed marriage.

It was as plain as the nose on Dara's face. And although she'd promised herself she'd always be here for him when he came home, this slap in the face broke all bargains.

Ripping free of Slim's light hold, she ran for the door, tugging at her wedding ring as she went.

"Dary, wait," he called after her. "Where do you think you're goin'?"

She responded with words she never thought she'd say. "I'm going home to Grandfather in San Francisco! I'm tired of loving a man who'll never love me back!" Shoving her ring into her jeans pocket where it clinked against Zane's, she hurried blindly through the doorway.

Zane pulled into the ranch yard, climbed out of the cab of the pickup truck and gazed around. There wasn't a vehicle in sight; the place looked deserted. Dara was probably over at headquarters visiting Kathy, he decided. She'd be back soon and when she arrived...

Nothing like a brush with death to make you appreciate what you had.

Whistling a little tune, he lowered the trailer ramp to unload his roping horse, working a bit awkwardly to favor the two broken fingers on his left hand.

The telephone line to Dara's grandfather's office was busy or broken or otherwise out of service. Standing at the open pay phone in Miller's Drugstore in Faraway, Dara tried calling his San Francisco mansion; Blythe would help her. But that call didn't go through, either.

Frustrated and miserable, she banged a fisted hand down on the instrument of this fresh disappointment. Her head drooped. Here she was, ready to concede defeat and there was no one available to hear her confession.

Silence pressed in upon her. She was on her own, she realized. If she gave up on her marriage, it would be her own choice and she'd never be able to blame it on her grandfather or anyone else. Almost unconsciously, she slipped a hand into her pocket to finger the two rings she carried there.

How touched and happy she'd been when Zane placed that ring on her finger! And when he'd slipped an identical band on his own finger, she'd felt that at last she was making progress with him.

She frowned, sensing that something wasn't quite right with the feel of the rings between her fingers. Pulling her hand from her pocket, she opened her fist to reveal two wedding bands, identical except for size.

Only they *weren't* identical anymore. One was no longer a perfect circle. In fact, she realized with a start, it looked as if it had been somehow *smashed*.

Instantly, her imagination took flight. What if some big animal had stepped on it in the rodeo arena—while it was still on Zane's finger? What if the ring had been pried off and dropped in the soft dirt? If that was the case, anything could have happened to it.

Including… Dara's eyes narrowed thoughtfully. Jody could have been there and just picked the ring up and put it in her pocket without saying anything to anyone. No one would have noticed.

But instead of thinking about Jody, Dara realized she should be thinking about Zane. Her stomach plummeted. If he'd been wearing this ring when it got bent out of shape, he could easily have been injured. In fact, the animal that did this could have done more, much more, than simply step on Zane's hand.

Her stomach clenched into a knot of dread. "Oh, God," she murmured to herself, "don't let Zane be hurt! If he's okay, I swear I'll never be jealous again…."

She had to know. No matter what it might do to her pride or her future, she had to be sure.

Slim lunged through the cabin door, looking completely frazzled. Zane, standing in the kitchen doorway eating a bowl of cold cereal, raised a quizzical brow.

"You picked a great time to come rollin' in," Slim stormed. "Why couldn't youa managed to get here a couple hours sooner?"

"What was goin' on a couple hours earlier that was so all-fired important?" Zane braced himself with his left hand on the door frame, favoring the two last fingers that were splinted and wrapped to twice their normal size.

"Jody Mitchell was happenin'," Slim said darkly.

"Huh?" Zane's stomach did a flip-flop and he frowned. "What's that supposed to mean?"

"That your ex-galfriend showed up to cause trouble and she did—boy howdy! At least, I'm a-hopin' she's a *ex*. The way she wuz talkin'…"

Zane's muscles tightened and he placed the empty bowl on a countertop before stalking toward the old cowboy. "You know there's been nothin' between me and Jody—hell, or any other woman—since I married Dara."

"Then why'd Jody come traipsin' in here with your wedding ring?" Slim challenged. "She threw it right in Dary's face. Up 'til then, I don't think Dary was buyin', but when she saw that ring, she looked like she was about to pass out." His voice became strident. "Why'd you take it off, Zane? Why'd you do that?"

"You old coot!" Zane clenched the only hand capable of such an action, raising the other to wave it around. "I didn't take it off. It was *took* off—by about a thousand pounds of steer stompin' on it. I spent hours crawlin' around that arena lookin' for that ring and now I know why I couldn't find it.''

"Because Jody beat you to it?'' Slim's eyes were wide and horrified.

"Looks like. Dara took this hard, you say?''

"Hard enough to light out in the Jeep.''

"Don't worry, she'll be back,'' Zane predicted, praying it was true. Otherwise, this was going to turn into the nightmare he'd always expected to have if he let a woman get under his skin. And Dara had. All his defensive tactics had failed and he suddenly realized that without her, he was lost. "Soon as she cools down—'' he began in a gravelly voice.

"Maybe, maybe not,'' Slim interrupted. "She said somethin' about callin' her grandpa.''

The bottom fell out of Zane's world. That could only mean one thing. "It's over, then,'' he said harshly. "I knew it couldn't last. Without love—''

"On your side, maybe,'' Slim declared. "She said she wuz tired of lovin' a man who don't love her back, and I gotta tell you, I cain't really find fault with that.''

A piercing pain shot through Zane and he shivered as if from a mortal blow. "She said *that?*''

"That she loved you? Yep.'' Slim grabbed the younger man by the shirt collar and gave him a good shake. "Wake up, cowboy! I know you! You got too damned much pride and you don't trust anything that's female, up to and includin' horses, but in this case you're dead wrong! If you coulda seen her, heard the crack in her voice…'' He paused to suck in a shaky breath. "If you'da been here, I'da punched you in the nose, I swear to God!"

"You like her a lot," Zane said, surprised by the depth of feeling he heard in the old man's passionate declaration.

"Yore dang tootin'! I been watchin' her tryin' ever which way she could to make you love her and I been tryin' to keep out of it. Now Dary's had enough and she's gone and you just stand there like a bump on a log…"

Slim ran out of breath and glared at his employer, whose feelings he'd completely misjudged. Zane *did* care; he cared desperately. Neither pride nor a lifelong fear of commitment was going to keep him from taking action. Reaching up, he gently removed Slim's hands from his shirt.

"Slim, old buddy, I'd advise you to stand aside until the smoke clears."

A great smile broke over Slim's face. "Does that mean what I think it means?"

"It means," Zane said, reaching for his hat on the peg beside the front door, "that I'm not givin' up without a helluva fight."

"Ya-hoo!" Slim's exuberant voice followed Zane toward the pickup. "Katy, bar the door!"

A good five miles from the cabin, Dara saw the plume of dust coming toward her. Had to be Slim, she surmised, heading into town for supplies. He'd probably be surprised to see her returning home, but so be it. She would swallow her pride this time.

The dirt road rambled along beside a split-rail

fence, beyond which spring wildflowers peeked through early greening grass. A brilliant sun shone overhead in a sky the color of a robin's egg, a few fluffy white clouds decorating the blue canvas.

My God, she thought, it's not enough that I love Zane, but I also love his country. Colorado is a wonderful place to live and it'll be a wonderful place to raise children—if I'm ever lucky enough to have any.

Despite all the trauma she'd gone through, she truly felt as if she was destined to spend her life here. Even if it didn't work out with Zane—that possibility brought a lump to her throat—she'd never go back to the life she'd lived in San Francisco.

But maybe it *would* work out; maybe Zane would have an explanation. No matter what it cost her, she was going to face him honestly and tell him—

The clamor of a vehicle horn blasted through her self-absorption and she slammed on the brakes in panic. A red pickup was bearing down on her. Pulling to the shoulder of the road, she stopped her Jeep and sat there breathing in great gasps, still clutching the wheel. What was the matter with that crazy driver? What was he trying to do, run her off the road?

The pickup skidded to a stop in a cloud of dust on the opposite side of the road. The driver's door flew open and a tall, lean figure jumped out and started running toward her.

Without stopping to think, Dara threw open her own door and flung herself forward to meet the man she loved halfway. They came together in the middle of the dirt road between two idling vehicles, crashing into each other's arms.

"You came back!" they said in unison, then shared nervous laughter. Zane dipped his head to kiss her, but she evaded his lips, knowing that if she didn't she'd never be able to say the things she had to say.

He held her away from him, a gleam in his fine dark eyes. "What's the matter? Aren't you glad to see me?" he challenged.

"I'm glad," she said breathlessly, "but there'll be none of that until we get a few things straight."

The corner of his mouth quirked down even as his grip tightened on her shoulders. "If this is about Jody, I can explain."

"This isn't about Jody," she gasped. "It's about you and me!"

He frowned. "But Slim told me Jody showed up and you got all bent out of shape and—"

"Stop it! I said this isn't about Jody." She covered his mouth with her fingertips to stop the misdirected flow of words, which was a mistake; he kissed them, nibbled on them. She drew her hand back quickly, sucking in a ragged breath. "Zane," she said in a determined voice, "I love you."

His dark eyes opened wide and his lips parted on a quick breath. When he started to speak, she again risked touching his mouth with her hand.

"Please, let me say it all before I lose my nerve." She licked her lips. "I don't know exactly when it happened, this way I feel about you, but I'm beginning to think it must have started that night in the Golden Gringo. Otherwise, why would I ever have married you, even considering how bad my state of mind was at the time?"

"I've wondered that myself," he said in a gruff voice.

"Yes, and I don't blame you for wondering," she agreed quickly. "You must have thought I was crazy to—"

"No, Dara," he broke in, "you don't understand. I wondered that about *myself.*"

She blinked; he'd broken her train of thought. "But—I'm sorry. Now I'm really confused."

"Then I'll clarify things for both of us—at least I'll try. You love me and I love you. I don't love Jody, never did, and at the moment I don't even like her much. And I sure as hell didn't give her my wedding ring or try to renew old acquaintances, if you get my drift."

"Oh, Zane." It came out an ecstatic sigh and she closed her eyes.

He must have misinterpreted, for he said in a suddenly anxious voice, "About my wedding ring…I really can explain. I had this run-in with a steer—"

"So it *was* a steer that stepped on your hand." She snuggled against his chest. "Any damage?"

"Broke two fingers but—hey!" He reared back so he could look down into her face. "You knew. Who told you?"

"Nobody. I figured it out all by myself." She added a bit anxiously, "Can I see?"

"Well, sure, but there's nothing much *to* see." Without releasing her completely, he offered his hand for her inspection.

"Ohhh…" She touched his wrist, looking down

with deep compassion at ragged bandages the size and shape of sausages.

"They said I'd live," he informed her dryly, pulling her back against his chest. "I was almost glad because it gave me an excuse to come home early."

"You needed an excuse to come home? Why?"

"Because I acted like a total…" He seemed to be struggling for a word that was both strong enough and yet socially acceptable.

"Jerk?" she suggested helpfully.

"I'll settle for that if you will." He sounded grateful. "It's just that when I came into the house and found you looking like a pinup centerfold, and all those wonderful smells coming from the kitchen…and then we made love—"

"It *was* love," she said quickly, "at least for me. I wanted to tell you. I *started* to tell you, but then Slim showed up." She let loose a little growl. "I wanted to strangle him for that!"

"He nearly strangled *me* when he confronted me about Jody. Honey, it was love for me, too, but I was afraid to admit it. All along I tried to be strong because…hell, I already cared too much. If you left me after we'd made love, I wasn't sure I could handle it."

"Zane Farley, you can handle anything!" She slipped her arms around his waist and kissed his throat. Tears trembled in her voice and she swallowed them back.

"Anything but losing you, Dara."

It was said with such a wealth of feeling that she knew it was true to the very depths of his being.

At last, she lifted her face for his kiss, finally secure in his love. How long they stood there kissing in the middle of the road, she had no idea, but it wasn't nearly long enough before the strident honking of an automobile horn brought her down off her cloud. Blinking, she peered around Zane's broad shoulder and saw yet another pickup, a twin to the Bar F vehicle Zane had left idling at the edge of the road.

Slim hung out of the window, a big grin creasing his face. "Hey, you two, you cain't stand around on a public road huggin' and kissin' like a couple a kids. Why don't you just get married and go on home like grown-ups?"

Dara laughed, but Zane's dark brows rose.

"That's a great idea." Dropping to one knee in the dust, he lifted Dara's hand between his own good hand and his bandaged hand. "Dara, will you marry me…again?" he asked with a seriousness that belied the gleam in his eyes. "I love you, pretty lady, and I want to spend the rest of my life—"

"Teaching me to ride a horse," she put in tartly.

"You mean that no-account Slim didn't teach you while I was gone?"

"I told you, I want *you* to teach me the things I need to know."

"I'm humbled," he said, "and that's a first." He kissed her hand. "So will you marry me or what?"

"I'll marry you," she said, adding with sudden inspiration, "on our first anniversary next December in Las Vegas, Nevada. And this time, you'll know exactly what you're doing and there'll be no excuses."

"No excuses for either of us," he agreed. "But

about Las Vegas—my chances of making the national finals this year are slim to none. This hasn't exactly been my best showing rodeowise. Wifewise..." He stood up and tilted her face so he could drop a light kiss on her nose. "I've already won the championship."

Slim cupped his mouth and shouted, "Told the two a you that it wuz fate. As for you, Zane Farley, I'm wonderin' why folks call you greased lightnin' considerin' how long it took you to catch on!"

When he drove away, they didn't even look up.

Zane and Dara Farley, the former Dara Linnell, renewed their marriage vows at sunset in Las Vegas the following December, despite the fact that for the first time in years, the bridegroom was an observer instead of a participant in the National Finals Rodeo. They were surrounded by friends and family: all the Farleys of Faraway, Colorado, and more surprisingly, by the Linnells of San Francisco.

Donald Linnell was still having a hard time with the whole thing, but apparently even he could see Dara's happiness. Relenting, he sat in the front row with his older granddaughter and her child, carrying a wedding gift in his pocket—a legal document relinquishing all control of Dara's trust fund. Now that he accepted the fact that she didn't care about the money in the slightest, it somehow became easier to give up control. Perhaps he'd do the same for Blythe, one of these days....

Among the many friends of the bridal couple, especially welcome were those who'd attended their first wedding exactly one year earlier. Instead of a sleazy, fast-food-type chapel, the happy couple held hands in a beautiful desert garden, landscaped with artful plantings of cacti laced with twinkling holiday lights.

Zane looked incredible in a dark, Western-tailored suit, and he'd put a lot of elbow grease into shining his boots. The bride dazzled well-wishers with her graceful cream-colored gauze gown, a replica of a Victorian summer dress. Slim served as best man and Kathy attended the bride.

The ceremony, everyone agreed, was lovely; there wasn't a dry eye in the house. When the minister pronounced them man and wife—again—they turned to each other with all the gladness of a couple who'd faced adversity and knew for sure that they belonged together, now and forever.

Suddenly, the bridegroom threw back his head and let out a whoop of joy that brought delighted smiles to those sharing this exquisite moment. Then, as if he couldn't contain his jubilation, he swept the bride up in his arms and twirled her around the garden—exposing the brown cowboy boots she wore beneath her gown.

In the front row, Shorty leaned forward to give Slim a thumbs-up while both applauded with gusto.

"That Dara is just about the purtiest bride I ever *did* see," Slim allowed.

"Yep," Shorty agreed in a stage whisper, "and don't ol' Zane just know it! He may not be rodeoin' here this week, but he's still got what it takes. Why, he grabbed her quick as greased lightnin'! If somebody'd had a stopwatch on him, he'd be the champion of the world for sure! Slim, old pal, it's fate, sure as shootin'."

The "old" newlyweds would have agreed.

MILLS & BOON®

Next Month's Romances

♡

Each month you can choose from a wide variety of romance novels from Mills & Boon®. Below are the new titles to look out for next month from the Presents™ and Enchanted™ series.

Presents™

FANTASY FOR TWO	Penny Jordan
AN EXCELLENT WIFE?	Charlotte Lamb
FUGITIVE BRIDE	Miranda Lee
THE GROOM SAID MAYBE!	Sandra Marton
THE MILLIONAIRE'S BABY	Diana Hamilton
MAKE-OVER MARRIAGE	Sharon Kendrick
THE SECRET FATHER	Kim Lawrence
WHEN DRAGONS DREAM	Kathleen O'Brien

Enchanted™

BERESFORD'S BRIDE	Margaret Way
THE FAKE FIANCÉ!	Leigh Michaels
A WEDDING IN THE FAMILY	Susan Fox
INSTANT MOTHER	Emma Richmond
RACHEL AND THE TOUGH GUY	Jeanne Allan
ANOTHER CHANCE FOR DADDY	Patricia Knoll
FALLING FOR JACK	Trisha David
MARRY IN HASTE	Heather Allison

On sale from 4th May 1998

H1 9804

DANCE FEVER

How would you like to win a year's supply of Mills & Boon®
books? Well you can and they're FREE! Simply complete the
competition below and send it to us by 31st October 1998.
The first five correct entries picked after the closing date will
each win a year's subscription to the Mills & Boon series of
their choice. What could be easier?

OBLARMOL
AMBUR
RTOXTFO
RASQUE
GANCO

KOPLA
OOOOMTLCIN
MALOENCF
SITWT
LASSA

EVJI
TAZLW
ACHACH
SCDIO
MAABS

G	R	I	H	C	H	A	R	J	T	O	N
O	P	A	R	L	H	U	B	P	I	B	W
M	O	O	R	L	L	A	B	M	C	V	H
B	L	D	I	O	O	K	C	L	U	P	E
R	K	U	B	N	C	R	Q	H	V	R	Z
S	A	N	I	O	O	N	G	W	A	S	V
T	S	I	N	R	M	G	E	U	B	G	H
W	L	G	H	S	O	R	Q	M	M	B	L
I	A	P	N	O	T	S	L	R	A	H	C
S	S	L	U	K	I	A	S	F	S	L	S
T	O	R	T	X	O	F	O	X	T	R	F
G	U	I	P	Z	N	D	I	S	C	O	Q

D8C

Please turn over for details of how to enter ⇨

HOW TO ENTER

There is a list of fifteen mixed up words overleaf, all of which when unscrambled spell popular dances. When you have unscrambled each word, you will find them hidden in the grid. They may appear forwards, backwards or diagonally. As you find each one, draw a line through it. Find all fifteen and fill in the coupon below then pop this page into an envelope and post it today. Don't forget you could win a year's supply of Mills & Boon® books—you don't even need to pay for a stamp!

Mills & Boon Dance Fever Competition
FREEPOST CN81, Croydon, Surrey, CR9 3WZ

EIRE readers send competition to PO Box 4546, Dublin 24.

Please tick the series you would like to receive if you are one of the lucky winners

Presents™ ❑   Enchanted™ ❑   Medical Romance™ ❑
Historical Romance™ ❑   Temptation® ❑

Are you a Reader Service™ subscriber?   Yes ❑   No ❑

Ms/Mrs/Miss/Mr ....Intials ....
                                    (BLOCK CAPITALS PLEASE)

Surname...

Address ....

....

....Postcode........................

(I am over 18 years of age)   D8C

Closing date for entries is 31st October 1998.
One application per household. Competition open to residents of the UK and Ireland only. You may be mailed with offers from other reputable companies as a result of this application. If you would prefer not to receive such offers, please tick this box.   ❑

Mills & Boon is a registered trademark of
Harlequin Mills & Boon Ltd.